Shadows of Dread

Matthew Dewey

Copyright

The Unsettling Subject

In the dark times, your body is put under extreme pressure. Stress levels are raised and rational thinking is thrown out the window. Eventually, this panic turns into true madness. It is no longer about fight or flight, it is about hiding the terrible truth to save you the pain. A trauma that does more damage than we can conceive.

In short, there is a point where your mind is no longer your friend. It is the false embrace of reassurance, the sweet lie to smother the horrible truth. The question is, what could drive someone to this point?

The year was 1938, a young man by the name of Maurice Robinson had his reality broken and his mind with it. He woke up screaming in his apartment. At first, the roommate thought someone had broken in and assaulted Maurice. With an empty beer bottle in hand, the roommate ventured into the darkness to find Maurice going from throwing fists at the air, to falling on his back, to shaking as if every muscle in his body was spasming, till he finally opened his eyes, quiet and calm.

The roommate told the police that Maurice was screaming 'no' at first, then he was begging. To add to the harrowing situation, a particular name was mentioned, one that was foreign to everyone who heard it, but familiar to people like me.

Gaurloskoth.

It is a name that was quickly erased from the records thanks to Julian Wright, an infiltrator under my employ. With charisma and manipulation, he ensured the police didn't think about the name but focus on another case instead. With any luck, the name will most likely be altered by fading memory or forgotten completely by those who heard it.

What matters now is Maurice.

Julien heard Maurice was to be taken to a mental institution, so he called us. Unfortunately, there were two major institutions in the city, Summerstone and Morningside. Such complications were difficult to handle, so I got everyone involved.

I sent Elliot and Bill to Morningside and Riley and Eliza to Summerstone. Later, we learned Summerstone was closed in 1927, over a decade ago, but the city records hadn't been updated. It would have been a problem if we didn't have Elliot and Eliza join us a week before.

The police arrived at Morningside with Maurice in the back of the car. He didn't struggle, he seemed catatonic. Guided by one officer straight into the hands of Elliot, who slowly guided Maurice toward the entrance until the police left. Once the police had turned the corner, Elliot and Bill gathered Maurice in their arms and carried him into their car. Perfect.

I sat that same evening in a dark observation room, watching Maurice through one-way glass. His eyes wandered here and there, a thousand-yard stare at all times. There wasn't much in the bare room for him to look at and it seemed like nothing would interest him if there were. It was saddening to see someone so broken. He seemed like a man down on his luck, with his last hope dashed. I had seen my father with the same look when my mother died, his eyes drifting from his drink to me, staring through me.

Yet, I would say Maurice only appeared that way. It felt like he knew he was in a room, but perhaps he saw more than I did. I realized this when his eyes drifted to me and focused. He stared straight into my eyes, which should have been impossible thanks to the one-way glass. In confusion, I cocked my head a little to one side only to have him mirror that movement.

That alone sent a shiver down my spine, which in turn made the dark room I was standing in feel a lot more...hostile. It was when Maurice mouthed what I thought was 'hello' that I felt something darker behind it all. Maurice didn't seem confused then, he was calm and confident. His look was condescending but mostly neutral. As if I were an ant, insignificant to him and my fate was of no consequence at all.

Maurice stared until he lost interest and his eyes drifted back to the corner of the room, a thousand-yard stare returning. It was a smooth, but fast change. My peace of mind didn't return so quickly, which is why I jumped when the door clicked and swung open to the observation room.

"Mr. Edwards, you called?" Elliot asked.

"Y-yes. Fetch the others, will you? I want them to watch as I interview the subject."

"Right away."

Elliot Ward left quickly. His readiness to obey orders only made me think of him less. Insubordination in most cases shows intelligence, that there is a brain behind those eyes. A brain that's constantly working, studying its superior, and evaluating their orders. I didn't get that impression from Elliot, not even a slight hesitation. He was a dog waiting for the stick to be thrown.

Elliot's sister, Eliza Ward, had the brains. I felt her judging eyes on me as soon as she entered the observation room with the others. Elliot and Eliza stood by each other, while the older part of my team, Bill, Riley, and Julian, stood closer to me. I explained that in my line of work, I need them to see for themselves what it was I dealt with. I needed them to see the importance of this work. With that, I left the observation room.

Stopping before entering the holding cell, I collected myself. A strong mind is needed in such situations, breathing helps keep me calm. With speed and confidence, I soon closed the door behind me and stared at the subject. Maurice remained, unmoving and cuffed to the fixed chair.

"Maurice?" I began, hoping to get his attention, as much as I could.

The subject simply stared into the distance. Only now, in his presence, I didn't pity him. Instead, my senses were detecting a threat. A voice at the back of my head kept repeating 'danger', but I only ignored it. That feeling of unease is common and expected in my line of work.

"Right, well, let's begin shall we?" I murmured, checking the cuffs around Maurice's wrists and legs. "Bill, the lights."

I looked up at the one-way mirror as I stood behind Maurice. For a brief moment, I thought they didn't hear me, but then the lights went out. The room wasn't thrown into pitch, but it was dark enough. The only light source now was the dim glow around the door frame. I could make out Maurice's shape, the faint lines outlining the one-way glass and even the walls.

The voice calling 'danger' grew a little louder.

"Gaurloskoth?" I asked the darkness more than I asked Maurice. "It's a name I am not familiar with...but I know the origin."

I didn't receive a response, Maurice was still.

"Gelkerot, does that sound familiar?" I continued, breathing deeply. "It's a name I know you're all familiar with. I would like to know if it's a name you fear or admire?"

Still no response. I needed to know now if I was barking up the wrong tree. If the reports were inaccurate, I could be talking to someone truly mad. Perhaps all that I saw before might have been a coincidence. Keep going/

"No, not Gelkerot? Perhaps...Remilotka?"

Nothing. I stared at the back of Maurice's silhouette and was disappointed. Walking past him, I made for the door. It was only when my hand clasped the handle that I noticed something different. The voices warning me before were now silent, yet...I still felt the undeniable presence of something.

"Gaurlo-" I murmured before I felt a pressure wrap around my throat.

My voice was silenced as a new voice filled the room. It was almost indescribable. Loud, yet soft. Weak, but strong. An anomaly of sound, but in every aspect, threatening. I felt it overpower my body and mind, I felt helpless.

"Remilotka is waiting for you, outsider."

I wheezed as I resumed control of my mind and quickly, my body as well.

As I took back control, I felt a falling sensation. My feet touched the ground and I breathed easily once more. It had lifted me off the ground and I barely noticed. Maurice, from what I could see, remained chained to his chair, but I wanted to make sure.

"Bill, lights."

The darkness was vanquished by the startling lights. I blinked quickly to regain focus, catching images that I barely understood before I saw them clearly. Maurice remained in the same position, staring sleepily at the corner of the room. Lowering my eyes, I saw the cuffs that chained him to the chair were still in place.

However, there was water beneath his chair. For a moment, I thought Maurice had relieved himself, then I saw the puddle recede, vanishing as if it were a fading spot in my vision. As it did, it gave me a headache. My sense of calm faded with it as I left the room. Once outside, I saw my team gathered in front of me. Only Julian and Bill seemed calm but concerned. The Wards and Riley had their eyes widened and skin pigment lightened.

When my eyes met Julian's, I could tell he understood the significance of the exchange as much as I did.

"Remilotka...why couldn't it have been Gelkerot?" I mumbled.

Realm of Remilotka

Finding a void god in this reality was difficult for me at first. The majority of research was done by a Frenchman named Hector Allaire, my ancestor. It is well-known that during the storming of the Bastille in July 1789, many valuables were stolen as well as prisoners freed. Among these valuables was a journal written by an 'insane' revolutionary, which was confiscated during his incarceration.

A peasant found the journal and brought it to Allaire, who paid well for it. Allaire became obsessed with this journal, famously so, but his interest did not spread far. A book was of little value to the common rabble that sought their freedom more than obscure, dark knowledge. Allaire's research was passed down through his family until it eventually reached me.

As far as I know, nobody in my family was interested in old documents and books. It was an obsession for me, then a profession, of my choosing. Still, having Allaire's research wasn't enough, which is why I took a holiday to France and made my way into the countryside, finding Allaire's grave. The journal rested on his chest. Even in death, he could not part with it.

The knowledge in that journal gave me all I needed to pass from this reality and enter theirs, however briefly. There, I learned more than I ever thought I would, saw more than I had ever seen. I discovered the true importance of my work. I am now responsible for protecting people from this...evil, for lack of a better word.

"However, I am only one man," I concluded. "The knowledge I found has cursed me, given me this burden and I am afraid to say I cannot bear it alone. I reached out to all of you not because you could help me snatch a possessed or acquire information, but because you have all experienced evil in some way. You have reasons beyond money and I ask you now to realize it."

I placed five vials of the silver solution on the low wall between me and my team. Even Julien eyed them with suspicion.

"I fear grim times are approaching and if you have read the papers you have the same fear, so consider this an ultimatum," I continued. "Joining me now will constitute a permanent partnership, as you will be just as trapped and freed as I am."

Once more I paused, observing their reactions. Eliza didn't seem so cool under such pressure, but she stood fast like everyone else.

"Those who do not join me will close their contract. You will receive your promised pay, but you will have nothing more to do with this work. Choose now."

To my surprise and delight, this was the signal they needed to act. Julien Wright, Riley O'Dunn, Bill Watts, and Elliot and Eliza Ward took their respective vials and drank with me. The cold chemicals flooded our system, feeling like smoke as it seemed to rise rather than fall and freeze like ice. It was almost numbing, but the exact opposite was true. Our minds were being strengthened and our senses heightened. It was a solution I feared to drink the first time I drank it, but after that time it was rather enjoyable.

Once downed, the solution made the cold night by the lake feel truly frigid. Yet, we didn't shake, not even a hair raised. A powerful calm indeed.

"What now, Mr. Edwards?" Elliot asked.

"Now, you can call me 'Morgan,'" I replied with confidence. "We are all bound together now, which I believe makes us friends."

We all exchanged semi-confident smiles before I turned to the lake.

"Here, cultists sacrificed hundreds of villagers to Remilotka, a void entity comparable to a god," I explained. "I say 'void' because Remilotka cannot exist in this reality, not yet anyway. Despite their gory deaths, it wasn't the blood that made this lake a shared point between this reality and theirs, it was simply the mass killing. Remilotka sensed it and used his power to tear a hole in both realities."

"And the...formula?" Eliza asked.

"The formula is one of the two things that makes it possible for us to see their reality," I explained. "It focuses our mind, strengthens it. Without it, we sense nothing out of the ordinary, and even if we could, we would most likely be driven as mad as Maurice."

"And the second thing?"

"Darkness. Make no mistake, these gods are the monsters that go bump in the night."

I walked from the car to the edge of the inky lake. The night was as bright as could be, with the stars shining and the moon full, but the lake was opaque.

"Follow me, call their names, question them, and get out when you need to," I told them. With one last look, before I entered the lake, I saw a determination in each of their faces.

These were scared people, people who wanted the same answers. For whatever reasons they had, I knew that by the end of the night, they would have the same feeling of responsibility as me.

We would be united by the same fear.

I plunged quickly into the lake as if pulled and was soon wrapped in a cruel mixture of sensations. The water took away any warmth, restricted my breathing, and soon I felt one with my body.

The darkness twisted in my vision as I walked along the lake floor, the water feeling less restricting with each step, the sound shifting in the same manner. It felt less like water by the second, till I could finally move freely, hear normally and I could even breathe safely. I had passed to a different reality, in almost every respect.

"Remilotka...I know you can hear...I know you can see me," I spoke into the darkness. "Now, make yourself known."

I sensed movement in the darkness. It wasn't the slight movement of a humanoid figure, it was the movement of a colossus. A creature of unimaginable magnitude had been disturbed. It made sense for Remilotka to be so close to a shared point in our realities, but I was still surprised by its presence.

Unlike Gaurloskoth, I didn't hear such an abnormal voice. Instead, I heard the familiar voices of all the important dead in my life speak in unison. A grim chant in the distance, almost a song of calling. I did not respond the way Remilotka expected.

"Gaurloskoth...I spoke to him," I murmured. "He told me that you're 'waiting' for me. I'm here now."

The chant grew louder. I heard children amongst the voices and I felt a warmth run down my cheeks. Still, my mind was unyielding even if the rest of me wasn't. Remilotka saw this and the chant disappeared into nothing. Its remaining echoes reverberated around me for a moment, till at last there was silence.

"Morgan?"

I closed my eyes, recognizing the voice. I heard the footsteps, the heels, and even her breathing. Opening my eyes again, I saw a figure in the darkness, a woman in a polka-dot dress. Her face showed loving concern, it made my heart warm, but my mind did not crumble. I stared with the same measure of determination my team showed before. The figure smiled cruelly and I watched it rot, melting into the darkness.

"Our reach is growing," her voice echoed around me. "You cannot stop the Second Visitation."

"You sound so sure," I muttered. "I wonder if you thought the same of the First Visitation?"

"We are undying, our time is inevitable."

"Undying...it must be a curse when you are stuck in oblivion."

There was no response from Remilotka, but another shaking movement in the darkness. I could see for the briefest moments the pale surface of a wall of skin.

"Silence...if only it were always this way," I murmured. "Doesn't matter, I heard enough. Remember this, monster, your prison is of your own making. Your kind is meant to suffer an eternity of darkness and I will make sure it stays that way."

As I walked in the direction of the lake's edge, I felt a tug as something tried to pull me back. I paused.

"Their kind is meant to cleanse," my mother whispered behind me. "They've seen other realities, destroyed other realities. Morgan...oh, my dear Morgan...submit."

Tugging my shoulder free of Remilotka's grasp, I sped onwards, feeling the weight of the lake and its cold embrace. For the briefest moments, as I broke the surface of the lake to breathe the night air, I had the childish fear that I would be pulled under. That I would be kept in his realm of horror, to drown or be driven mad.

I snapped out of this grim mentality as the rest of my team broke the surface of the water. I saw in their wet, disturbed faces the same sense of fear I felt the first time I came face-to-face with the eldritch beings. Their collective terror seeped into my body, breaking my courage down piece-by-piece until my mind broke with it.

We all stumbled back onto land, our wet clothes clinging to our bodies. With our dripping forms and new perspective, we were born again. Although, there was nothing holy about this rebirth, quite the opposite.

"Everyone...you have seen it for yourself," I announced. "The powers that threaten our world, our children, their children, and so on until the end of time."

"H-how...how can we fight?" Riley asked. "These beasts, they're beyond you or I and that's an understatement if I do say so myself and I do!"

"No, Riley, you are wrong. It's been done before and it will be done again. I don't know what it is you all saw, but no doubt you heard the same thing. You heard this fight is pointless?"

Each one avoided my eyes, staring at their feet or staring off into the distance.

"I see it in your eyes," I whispered, anger filling my voice. "I see the crippling fear that breaks most weak minds, that destroys one's spirit, but believe me when I say I know that won't be you!"

I grabbed Eliza, whose eyes had stared too far into the darkness of the forest behind me. Shaking her as I spoke, I saw her gaze refocus on me.

"You have all seen hell before!" I continued. "It did not take you and neither will this. Eliza, Elliot, you saw the horrific death of all you held dear at your weakest and you didn't falter."

I turned to Julien next.

"You ran across the bodies of those who fought beside you, through a rain of death for what you knew was right," I murmured, next turning to Bill. "You experienced the cruelty of a mad mind and it fueled you to bring justice. You saved me when I was so young, I know first-hand you have no fear.."

At this, Bill smirked, the others smiling with him.

"And you, Riley," I spoke confidently. "Despite being the youngest of us, you are no stranger to evil. You may not have known it then, but you were beaten down by these monsters. You got up and said-"

"An O'Dunn fights till his last and you best believe it," Riley grinned, his roguish personality showing itself once more. "So, what's the plan, boss?"

The answer wasn't an easy one to give. We would never get answers from a void god, nor could we risk going mad by entering their realm so many times. We would need to fight them from our reality, which meant finding out how they were combatted in the past. Unfortunately, our side of the fight hasn't done well in keeping that history intact.

I knew what we needed to do, but the time wasn't right.

"There's nothing we can do now," I told them. "Not in this climate anyway. War is on the horizon and no matter where any of you end up, realize that you have another mission. I will call on all of you again. I don't know when, but all I ask is that you be ready."

The End of Daniel Morris

Morris House was quiet that evening. Daniel Morris examined the paper close to the fire, reading with concerned eyes. A tale of evil was plastered across the page, describing the deaths at Bennet Manor in another part of the country. By the end of the paper, once he learned all the servants at the Manor had been executed, Daniel shook his head and threw the paper into the fire.

"Dear, why are you still up?" Jane Morris murmured from the dark, wearing her a flowing gown. "What's wrong?"

"Nothing, it's nothing!" Daniel snapped. "Why do you insist on wearing that thing? You look like the Lost Bride when you drift in here!"

Jane scowled across the room, the daggers from her eyes piercing Daniel's, but she said nothing in reply. Daniel watched as his wife's dress flowed as she retreated to her bedroom. As she left, silence returned and Daniel calmed with it. Grimacing at the thought of himself, Daniel decided to warm himself beside another hearth.

Collecting his coat, Daniel ventured into the night, cursing his name and those associated with it.

"If I didn't get it from my father, I got it from my mother," Daniel spat. "If not the pair of them, then the witches of hell that I call my sisters! You are the ones who drove me to madness and even in peace, I find myself suffering. If any of you were alive...you would surely seek to prolong my suffering and take away all which does make life bearable."

A thought Daniel hated, but it was true. Even in death, his family haunted him in memory and life. The house was left to him, with not a single penny to maintain it. A wife, presented by his mother to wed and love for a bitter eternity. Even the face he wore was not his own, as he bore an extraordinary likeness to his father.

Whatever was truly Daniels was not worth mentioning. Instead, if he could not find peace with himself, he would find peace as someone else. Daniel's eyes widened as the thought crossed his mind, so it returned and in full force. With the illogical thoughts that one inherits from the darkest time of night, Mr Daniel Morris began to fade and a new persona began to take control.

Daniel's steps were smoother, as his stride grew confident. The smile upon his face was twisted, as his muscles fought to smile in a way he never did. From the way Daniel held himself to the way he studied every individual that passed him, he became less himself.

And very soon, he lost himself to a new spirit.

*****

"Are you sure?" Jane Morris asked. "I mean, it's rather odd for the two of us to be at sea again. I still have no idea how to swim!"

"The captain assures me that it will be calm, my love," Daniel kissed her forehead. "I think it's time we took advantage of all the time we have now in our old age to reconnect. What place is better than where we first met?"

Jane smiled softly at the thought of Daniel in his sailor's uniform. The thought of how tall he was back then, how strong. The feeling of being wrapped in his arms and then lifted and carried. Sharing smiles constantly. Yet, that was a different time, when they were different people. The smile disappeared and Jane eyed her aged husband.

Jane Morris wanted to go home.

The captain of the Sanguine Finch greeted the passengers as they boarded. People of all ages, but Jane and Daniel Morris were by far the oldest. Their pale complexions, their deep wrinkles, and white hair set them out clearly amongst the rest of the passengers.

Although, the captain had to admire the way Daniel carried himself. He stood tall, chest out, and almost seemed to march. Even his commanding officer didn't show such vigor and strength in his demeanor upon reaching such an age.

"Good to have you, Mr. and Mrs. Morris," the captain greeted. "I must say, Mr. Morris, you appear in great spirits."

"It's a fine day to be at sea, captain," Daniel saluted casually. "Tell me, would you mind giving an old sailor a tour of the helm?"

"No, not at all," the captain replied, pleasantly surprised. "We can discuss it further once everyone's aboard."

Daniel nodded smartly and marched on up the gangplank with his wife's arm hooked around his. Jane still studied her husband with curiosity, but even she was affected by his positive energy. Soon, at dinner, she would write it off as a change of heart. A side of her husband she had not seen since their marriage began and upon further thought, she found herself the smaller person for not replying in kind.

"Darling, do you mind if I join the captain?" Daniel asked Jane.

"O-oh, please, don't let me keep you," Jane smiled awkwardly. "Have fun!"

Watching Daniel walk away left Jane feeling saddened, another situation she remembered fondly from her younger days. It was overpowering her to such an extent, she couldn't stand to be in the dining area any longer. Instead of joining the droves of people retiring to their rooms, she decided to stay out in the night air. With a light heart, Jade Morris looked out at the dark sea.

A relaxing moment disturbed by the deep sigh beside Jane. Many thoughts crossed her mind and none of them was pleasant. For a moment she thought it was a snake or perhaps steam escaping some pipe. Yet, she found only her husband looking tired and upset.

"Daniel? What's wrong?"

"It appears the captain has taken ill, the tour was cut short."

"It's a shame, but I am sure you will have another chance next time. When do we return?"

"The ship docks at eight. Come, let's wait in our cabin until-"

"It must be nearing eight, why isn't the captain heading to shore?"

"The captain knows what he is doing."

"Well, you've sailed, what is he-"

Jane's questions began to unravel the mask. In the cool light, Daniel Morris's face did not appear to be his own. He stared wide-eyed, youthful, and angry. It was a flash of wrath, but in a flicker, it disappeared and the calm nature of her husband returned. However, that moment was enough for Jane to hesitate once more when Daniel stepped closer.

"Jane, what's-" Daniel began, but her eyes showed nothing but fear.

That fear alone gave the entity a joy it relished. A fear that it had seen moments earlier when it demonstrated its will on the captain. A fear that fuelled it to demonstrate more as it reached into its pocket and drew a dining knife.

***

"'...believed to have drifted off to sea or sunk in a storm, the search for the Sanguine Finch was called off on the 12th of July.' It's a shame, Finch was always packed with people."

"I'd say it was the captain."

"What are you talking about?"

"You know, the captain. He must have done it, wiped 'em all out in one fell swoop!"

"Show some respect, I knew the guy."

"Me too."

"Same here. He was a good man, a strong man. Even during the war, he was calm and as steady as his sailing. I say, if there was foul play, someone else did it."

"I can believe that."

"Hey, hey! Why does someone have to be a killer? It could have been an accident, a tragedy."

"Well, why not a killer? It's fun to think that something scary happened out there. The best stories are exaggerated anyway. Let's...hey, listen to this..."

Those that didn't gather around still listened as the man spoke. Taking in every detail of the story he began to weave and despite its impossibilities, they continued to listen and imagine.

The Summons

Mankind lives in a time where everything is known. What little they don't know is considered irrelevant in the grand scheme of things. Everyone has their minds geared towards the future, towards progress. This is why, when the incident transpired, nobody had an answer for what happened. It was beyond their realm of thinking, their researched reality.

Hector Glass, an old mechanic, was working on his truck. The blue sky, blotted with gray clouds here and there, soon darkened. Time passed so quickly that when he looked up from the leaking filter he wrenched from his truck, he was shocked. He placed the filter on the table, turned off the barn light, and with great effort, closed the two heavy doors.

The mechanic walked leisurely back to his house, surveying the countryside as he walked. The sun finally fell below the horizon, leaving only a green-purple light across the sky. Pushing his front door open, Hector called for his wife. After no response, he simply followed the sound of voices to the living room.

Agnes Glass sat in her large chair, a small, frail woman falling asleep. The drama that played on the old tv-set went unheard as her eyes finally shut before Hector entered. He saw Agnes drifting away, hand-in-hand with Morpheus, to a dream world he could never visit. He smiled fondly, examining her kindly features as he sat in the chair beside her. He knew he had to wake her, but he wanted to give her a moment's peace.

Mrs. Glass was different from other wives, who would throw a fit at their husbands for missing the dinner they prepared with love. Agnes simply understood how Hector could lose himself, becoming deaf, blind, and dumb to the world. A plate of cold food sat on the coffee table in front of them and Hector began to eat gratefully.

A peaceful moment, silence disturbed only by the crackling voices that came from the television. When Hector found himself slipping as well, he pushed himself out of his seat and made to wake Agnes. Before his hand could even touch her shoulder, a flash of movement caught his eye.

Hector froze, staring out the window for a long moment. In a dark room with only the white light of the television behind him, Hector could only make out the reflection of the room in the glass. Staring at his dark form, Hector sighed thinking of the worst.

Leaning down, Hector shook Agnes awake. When her eyes fluttered open and saw her husband, Agnes tried to say something but was quickly silenced by a warm hand over her mouth. Without a word, Hector guided his wife out of the living room and towards the stairs. It was slow as they had no lights to help them and fear kept Hector from turning any on.

Despite the difficulty, Hector and Agnes soon reached their bedroom. Hector sat his wife down in the bed, whispering what he saw to her, telling her to wait while he looked outside. There was no argument, but once Hector closed the door as he left, Agnes plucked up the telephone and began to call the police. To her dismay, the line was dead. She looked out the bedroom window, a creeping fear building inside her heart.

Hector had only an old shotgun and a dusty box of cartridges to keep his home secure. With it in hand, he felt more secure leaving his home to investigate the fields. Hector was not a farmer, he didn't grow crops and keep livestock, only fields of grass and the odd tree surrounded his home. Watching over his land, from the porch of his house, he was able to spot movement in the distance.

Scowling, the old man marched towards the crawling figure. It didn't appear to have noticed him, far too concerned with something in the grass. Had he been further away, the form would have appeared to be a dog or some other four-legged creature scavenging. As Hector would soon discover, the form was not as human as he believed.

It lifted its small head on a long neck, turning towards the light of Hector's flashlight. The pale, white eyes gleamed in the light, the jaw swinging from the skull with the sudden movement as if the being's lower face was melting from its skull. The pale complexion, the ragged clothing, and the monstrous appearance had Hector confused as well as terrified.

The thought of a creature like this, so close to his home that he could see it crawling in the dark from his window, made Hector Glass's heart sink and his blood cold.

Before Hector could say a word or raise his gun to fire a warning shot, the ground shook. The earth cracked, the world trembled beneath Hector and he fell unable to keep his balance. It was an earthquake unlike any he had ever experienced and at the worst time. He pushed himself off the ground, trying to keep his balance. Yet, all he could do was watch as the crawling creature fled.

Hector tried to follow, but could only manage a few steps before he tripped. It was not the rumbling ground that brought him down, but the assortment of objects laid out on the grass. Hector had only a moment to glance at them, seeing odd stones with carvings he could not examine properly and even the corpses of small animals, from rodents to rabbits.

Confused and scared, Hector remembered his wife and looked down at the lone house down the hill. Clambering to his feet, he marched down as fast as he could toward his home. He could see a window break in all the shaking and he cursed the idea that something could have fallen on Anges. The earthquake didn't lessen, instead, it grew stronger with each passing moment, until at last, the ground opened up.

Hector stopped in place, watching the earth separate, a divide between him and his home spanning wider and wider. The dirt rumbled and a loud crack as the rocks split. It was catastrophic and all Hector could do was watch. Watch as the land he stood on carried him further away from his home. He screamed her name, but it was muffled by the noise.

The land began to sink away, taking the barn along with Hector's truck. For a moment, Hector feared that his home would fall into the chasm with it, but his fear subsided when it finally ended. The ground stopped shaking, the noise faded and as quickly as it all began, it ended. The silence of the night returned.

Hector Glass saw his house stand strong and then the sight of his wife Agnes, standing at one window. She looked out across the chasm and saw her husband. Hector fell to his knees once more, but this time it was of his own will. Grateful that what was important still existed, grateful that his heart could take all the excitement.

Yet, it was only the eye of the storm.

From the chasm came a thunder, not of cracking rock, but of voice. A roar, a cry of anger. It asked of the world, in a voice so powerful that it shook Hector and Agnes to their core, it asked who had woken it. Hector dared not approach the edge to make sense of it, his legs could not move. However, it did not matter, as from the dark pit a hand greater than any other, larger than the home he lived in, stretched towards the sky, only to fall and grasp the edge of the chasm.

The force was tremendous, bending the earth and causing Hector to jump as the tremor ran through him. Another hand followed and then the fierce head of the titan. Its wizened face is made cruel by its snarling expression and long white hair and beard. The ground struggled to hold firm, eventually crumbling beneath his grasp. The giant clutched, scrambling to stay above ground, but to no avail.

In the chaos, the earth was wrenched in mighty handfuls, only to fall into the pit. Hector Glass followed the monster as the ground gave way. As if recognizing the horror it nearly unleashed, the earth began to close. The ground trembled once more, closing the chasm until at last the earthly prison was shut.

Agnes Glass, who fainted at the sight of something she could not explain, was woken up by the police. Without a single memory of what happened after the earthquake began, she thought her husband had fallen into the chasm that swallowed the barn. No matter what remembered, or how the police tried to make sense of it, there would always be lingering horror at the back of Agnes's mind.

A horror that Mrs Glass's mind would not dare recall, preferring to preserve itself in denial, than to suffer in fear. She would still live in that home, unaware of the creature that returned. A creature twisted by an ancient evil. A creature bent on recreating the ritual that broke the earth and released its master.

Corrupted

There used to be a time when creating life was considered both impossible and immoral. A crime against nature, a line that nobody would cross. Yet, as with most lines, it is eventually crossed. The creation of synthetic life was met with both looks of wonder and horror. The first official robot equipped with human-like AI inspired the world and a new era began. Yet, the true first synthetic life remained buried in conspiracy and legend.

Professor Ozrin watched from his broken home as the world celebrated the first instance of man-made life, cheering in crowds as the entity gave a powerful speech, filled with human error, but also heart. Tears were wept and they disgusted the professor. With animalistic fury, he clutched the holo-projector, throwing the delicate instrument through his apartment window. It was dissatisfying to see the window dematerialize as the projector flew through the frame and reappeared once it had passed.

Yet, the sound of the projector smashing on the pavement gave him some cathartic pleasure.

"Dakon?" Ozrin drunkenly called. "Dakon?!"

"M-master, I'm here," Dakon responded from the corner of the room, where he had been huddled. Darkness clouded him, but the blinking lights from his metallic frame hinted at the horror that was his rotting, human face. "I've been here since you told me, since Tuesday."

"I know what I said!" Ozrin yelled, causing Dakon to shake.

The human reaction infuriated Ozrin further. He remembered begging the Synthetic Institute to review his creation, but they simply showed him the door. He understood now. He understood how they were in the process of creating their own synthetic life and thanks to their standing claimed all the glory.

"Nobody remembers the second man to step on Mars," Ozrin stepped towards Dakon. "Nobody...I gave my life, all I had!"

Ozrin clutched the closest wine bottle, smashing it against the wall. He held in his hand the instrument that would bring about Dakon's demise. With a jagged glass in hand, Ozrin approached Dakon who could only watch in childlike fear.

Ozrin paused.

"D-Dakon?" Tears fell down Ozrin's cheek. "Dakon, I hate you…"

Ozrin fell forward, his body convulsing as a current ran through his body. The mangled form of one of Ozrin's older experiments had crawled across the ground and clutched Ozrin's leg. The twisted creature was a failed experiment, not destroyed, but dying. It's one human eye twitched as it studied Dakon. Metal parts that would move its mouth moved as if it were speaking to Dakon, but no words came out.

Unfinished, unable to speak its dying thoughts, Dakon could only watch as it crawled on top of Ozrin, plunging the jagged stump that would be its left arm through Ozrin's heart. As satisfied as it could be in his new form, the entity died with his memories of when he was still a whole man. Finally, it felt content having taken his revenge.

Dakon watched as the last spark of life faded as if flowing from the form with its black blood.

Dakon could not stay put, horror and disgust playing hell with his fragile mind. He collected clothing, covering his strange form, but most importantly, his decaying face. Dakon could not even bear to look in a mirror directly, choosing to create a mask from the parts from Professor Ozrin's lab. With the electrical charges in his metal mind wreaking havoc, Dakon fled into the apartment hallway.

A young couple had been passing the door, both shocked by the terrifying, masked figure and then horrified by the sight of the deceased professor. Dakon was already running away before the couple could do the same. Panic was detected, true horror and desire to contact the police. Sensors went off and the authorities alerted. Before Darkon had reached the stairs the police were already on route.

Dakon had a sense of survival, not to mention an abnormal life signature. He disappeared, practically undetected, into the night.

***

Twenty years had passed. The world had become something out of a science fiction writer's dream. Developments in every field skyrocketed productivity and decreased the value of luxury. Most could enjoy the safety of their home, protected by all manner of forces, from human to robotic. Everyone could enjoy the many pieces of technology that made life so wonderful.

With poverty, hunger, and homelessness nearly eradicated, the streets seemed so empty. Below these silent roads was an underground utopia, filled with the waste and rodents that society created. Among the shadows and rats, was the seated figure Dakon, who scratched at the rust on his arm.

Nobody sought him, he could not be found. In the sewers, he was safe, in the sewers he was king. His face was now bone, as the last of his mortal flesh had rotted and fallen away. Now, he saw with only a single mechanical eye, as the other had been taken by a rat long ago. He wondered when he would die when something essential for his survival would finally give out. Yet, all that seemed to break or waste away was unnecessary. Even the power that ran through him seemed unlimited.

In the two decades, he had to ponder his existence, and what he was compared to both human and synthetic life. Even the term cyborg didn't fit him, as all that was human had died long ago. With sadness, an emotion that caused his left leg to twitch, Dakon limped onwards through the sewers. Rats used to follow him, which gave him a measure of comfort, but without flesh, they now ran away.

Eventually, Dakon reached a grate that gave a clear view of the glowing city. The bright lights, the hum of power. Billboards flickered in and out of existence, advertising the latest and greatest humanity had to offer. Mostly it was synthetic life, so 'human' you could not tell the difference. Yet, Dakon knew that if you were to tear one open you would find the same parts that made him.

Dakon found himself thinking about it more and more until eventually, an idea spawned from his desperation and desire. With a mask and old clothing covering his disturbing form, Dakon left the sewers, joining the masses of people in the morning. He even wandered through the same neighborhood he was created, staring up at the building that he once lived in. If there was still a slum in the new world, it was there. A decaying building, holding nothing but bad dreams and worse memories.

Dakon continued his journey.

He could not very well speak to anyone and ask them the questions on his mind. The thoughts he had might be blurted out, so he had to make sure he found one. He had to make sure it was synthetic. It wasn't too long before he overheard a conversation on the street that piqued his interest.

"...not too different from a hospital for humans. We have doctors, but more bioengineers than medical doctors."

"And do you ever get sick?"

"Well, a disease is not too different from a computer error. It can cause damage to a system and so on. We inevitably run into problems, like moving slower or an error in our core. That's why we all cough the same. When we cough, it is our system telling us that we have a problem. Most of the time rest, or an update, does the trick. Otherwise, we go to the hospital."

The conversation continued for a few minutes longer. The human kept asking the synthetic questions it had no problem answering. Yet, as it spoke, you could tell it was growing impatient. Dakon could only admire how well synthetics were developed, while he still lacked much of what the synthetic was talking about.

Dakon approached the synthetic once it was alone, hunching himself over and pretending to struggle as he walked. He caught the synthetic's attention but noticed the eyes water and nose quiver in disgust. Dakon was not aware of his smell, yet he continued with his plan. He asked the synthetic to help him get through an alley toward his home, saying he was afraid of falling before he reached the door.

Dakon's voice was childlike, programmed so long ago to be so high and innocent. Yet, this only made the synthetic pity Dakon more. The two walked away from the busy streets, taking darker turns, one after another. By the time the synthetic began to worry if he should keep helping Dakon, Dakon attacked.

The fight was short. Dakon knew how they were built, he knew where to strike. Before the synthetic could react, Dakon's hand had reached into the synthetic's chest, parting the flesh with ease and clutching at what had to be vital. With machine-like efficacy, the synthetic was on the ground, silver blood pouring from its chest. It could only watch, paralyzed, as Dakon began to take it apart.

Dakon wasn't an animal, he deconstructed the synthetic with as much care as was necessary. With his knowledge and robotic movements, it was an easy process and soon the synthetic lay in pieces. Dakon began to work on himself, taking what he could and making it a part of himself. Some parts would be too risky to replace, but it didn't matter. What mattered was the feel and appearance he had.

The day seemed to pass so quickly but by the end of it, Dakon had stolen the synthetic's identity. The outer appearance had only one difference, the eye Professor Ozrin gave him. The broken synthetic remained on the ground, unmoving and still alive. In its mental hell, it watched as Dakon stood within view, examining himself in the reflective surface of his mask. It smiled, although it was robotic.

The synthetic wanted to scream, but nothing could save him at that moment.

Dakon didn't look back at the synthetic, instead, he donned the new clothes and left to join the society. With no ties to the new world, Dakon could do as he pleased and go where he wished. He had a human appearance but lacked every human error. Although not perfect, his core was reliable and it would not fault him.

The synthetic would be discovered, although dead and unable to recall what happened to it when revived. Dakon would not be discovered, blending seamlessly into the new world, in search of a place. If he failed to find his place, he would take that too.

Night Call

Now, I would like to state, for the record, that I had no involvement in the matter other than the fact that I discovered the body, okay? I reported it to the police straight away, in person and without going anywhere near the room upon finding my employee.

Do you understand that? Good.

Now, let me tell you why I believe that this was the work of a lunatic that has been harassing our store for the past month.

Just after the fifth or so, we began receiving calls late at night. We run a twenty-four-hour business, you understand? We don't often get calls, as you can tell from our call history, but we do get them. Strangers pitch up; we fill the car with gas and send them on their merry way.

Occasionally we get the fool who tries to make a run for it without paying, but ever since we set up those automatic blockers, they can't pull stunts like that. However, this caller is far worse.

He would harass Sally, the poor girl. She worked hard and it was the last thing she needed. I knew...well, still know her family and they were scared when she told them about this psychopath.

The man spoke right up to the phone, just filled with static, spit, and venom. "A real dirtbag." was what we first thought, but the next night shift she had we received another call from him. It was at this point we realized he knew Sally's schedule and was taking advantage of it.

I honestly considered changing my shifts so I would be there with her during her night shifts, but she was the one who told me not to bother. She felt confident enough to look after herself and not to mention our mechanic was working that night too, rest his poor soul. I didn't even know he was another victim until your officers brought it to my attention.

Sorry, what was that? No, I don't think he had any involvement either. He was a little shifty, but he was hill-folk. Trust me when I say he wouldn't hurt a butterfly, directly or indirectly. His voice didn't match the psycho either. What? I can't use that word? Well, that's exactly what he is, a psychopath; a terrible, murdering, psychopathic monster.

Now, where was I...? Ah, right, that night I did receive a call to my house phone from Dale, the mechanic who told me that he needed to order a part and needed my permission. I shouted at him of course, it was too late at night to receive a call like that. I made to hang up, but soon I heard something else over the line. It was Sally and the two were arguing. I only heard a brief snippet, something about the phone, probably her telling him not to call me; then he hung up.

Now, once more, I would like to say that Dale is harmless and wouldn't hurt a fly. He certainly wouldn't hurt Sally because we shouted at him; he is far too used to that. However, what raised my suspicions is when you showed me the call history. That night we didn't receive a call from the lunatic. After receiving so many calls from the psycho I found that incredibly unusual. I'm not telling you how to do your job or anything, but I highlighted the caller number and you could trace him through...

"Sir, thank you for your information," the county officer interrupted, holding up his hands to calm me down. "However, when it comes to tracing numbers, we often fall short of public expectations if I am being honest. We are not your CSI show but don't worry. The case is incredibly sensitive and has raised a lot of attention, as you can imagine. We are dedicated, like with all cases we receive, to resolving them and bringing the criminal to justice. I hope you understand."

"Of course, I know that this must be very little to go on," I nodded, feeling an age-old click in my neck. I rubbed it and grunted the annoying pain away. "However, as I said, I know the family and feel partly responsible for what has happened to my employees. Whatever assistance I can give you I will gladly give."

"That's great to hear," the officer nodded with a half-smile, taking the phone history from the table and putting it in his desk drawer. "Now, not to be rude, but..."

"Oh, don't worry, I will leave now," I murmured politely, standing up and heading to the door, passing an assortment of other people waiting to talk to the police.

As I reached for the doorknob, I heard the ring of a phone behind me. I turned my eyes from the sight of the dark outside back to the officer's desk. He plucked the phone and held it to his ear. He noticed I was still in the room and watching him with perhaps a hint of worry. The officer smiled and gave me thumbs up as he began talking with what was either another civilian or colleague.

I don't know what made me so tense, but I pushed it out of my thoughts and climbed into my old pickup. I put it in gear and was soon traveling in and out of streetlights on my way home. It was only around halfway that I once more heard ringing.

Ringing all around me; upon further investigation, I found that there were several phones in my car. One in the glove box, below my seat, at the pedals, under the passage seat, and several I could hear in the back. I was terrified, but the moment I answered one, they all stopped.

"Enough is enough, I am still here, stop talking, stop talking, stop talking about me," the familiar, spine-melting voice spat into the phone.

I didn't know what to say to him. He just continued to chant the words, 'stop talking' and realized he must have seen me leave the police station.

"I will stop," I murmured back, fear showing so clearly in my weak voice.

"He says he will stop, but of course, he won't," the voice groaned to someone else. "So many people talk about me now, so many, so many, so many people talking about me!"

My breathing became suddenly erratic and I hung up. For a painful still moment, my body and mind froze, wondering if that was a good thing to do.

I felt a cool breath on the back of my neck.

"Do you really think I'm a psychopath?"

Cold Hands

For us, the house was home. Sure, it was small compared to most houses, but it had plenty of rooms, even an attic. The door had a strange squeak which I found charming, the walls were well-painted and the plumbing worked. Overall, moving here seemed like a fantastic idea, especially to me at first, which is why I can see why my family found it confusing that I now live in fear of the place.

For two weeks since we arrived we were unpacking in a frenzy. I have a brother and we were told to choose our rooms. Our parents thought it would result in us having a logical discussion, but instead, it was a dangerous race up the stairs to the most desired room. Of course, being both boys our aggression was truly shown and as my brother reached for the doorknob ahead of me, I tackled him to the ground.

Our battle was brief because we were soon separated by our father who reminded us of the best way to decide who gets what. No, not a discussion to see who had more logical reasons to live in the room; instead we use the classic method of rock, paper, scissors. Unfortunately, it didn't go my way, probably karma for my aggressive behavior, but I honestly accepted it quickly. Whatever rock, paper, scissors says goes.

With that, I moved up the hallway to the adjacent room and began unpacking. Those two weeks I actually enjoyed, until at least it came to the day when we had to clean out the attic. On that weekend we were led by our father up a shaky ladder into the attic space. I never fully understood how stuffy a room could become until I entered the attic. You could almost taste the age of the air.

The three of us cleaned out boxes caked in stuff that looked like it was straight out of a science-fiction lab. It was dust and mold of such strange color you would think we were in another world. Once a majority of the old junk had been cleared out, we discovered what appeared to be a violin. Now, nobody in our family was particularly musical or even musically inclined. We looked it over and I knew my dad was wondering how much it would sell for. Of course, that had to wait as we were still busy throwing out the old resident's junk and moving ours in.

It didn't take long for the violin to pass from my family's minds, but it stuck around in mine. As I stated before, we are not musically inclined, but my curiosity about the violin was clear. I would stare up at the trap door of the attic every time I passed beneath it to go to my room. I would wonder what the sound would be like if I actually did play it. It was a curiosity I was sure would pass, but even after a month of thinking about it, this curiosity wasn't going away anytime soon.

I found that I wasn't just curious about the violin, it was curious about me. We were all heading towards our rooms to prepare for bed, climbing the stairs and taking turns in the bathroom. Of course, I was last, because scissors beat paper. As I waited outside the door my eyes shifted back towards the attic trap door to discover it was open and the ladder had descended.

I would have thought it was someone in my family that was up there, but I knew full well where each member was, so it couldn't have been them. For the longest moment, I felt like climbing the ladder and taking another look, but I was young. Even I am not ashamed to admit that the idea of climbing into a dark attic terrified me. I reached the foot of the ladder and pushed it upwards till the mechanism clicked and the ladder was pulled up, shutting the trap door.

I waited a little longer, brushed my teeth, and went off to my room. The look on my face, when I saw the violin on my desk chair, must have been priceless because I backed away from it in surprise. It sat there, out of the case with the bow resting on the armrests of my chair. I didn't question it as much as I should have; instead, I walked straight up to it and held it. What I found at first strange was that the violin felt warm, but I soon realized that was in contrast to my hands. My hands felt deathly cold and I immediately placed the violin down so I could breathe into them.

Eventually, there was some semblance of warmth, but it passed like a flick of the switch. There wasn't much I could do about them, so I picked up the violin, seeing as it felt warm in my hands, and tried playing a note. The moment the bowstrings touched the violin strings I saw a puff of gray smoke drift off them. At first, I thought it might have been dust from all its time in the attic, but I could indeed smell burning.

Sliding the bow along the strings again, more smoke appeared and once more a noxious smell of fire filled my nostrils. Due to the smell and discomfort in my cold hands, I placed the violin down and went to bed, having done more than my courage could take. As I climbed into bed I was shocked by the coldness in my hands. I stared at them intensely and saw that they were turning pale and then a shade of purple-like blue. Worry immediately flooded my mind and I left the bed, running to the bathroom.

I turned on the tap and let the hot water run. Its steam began to fill the room and I held my hands beneath it. Despite my best efforts, the cold continued and my hands stayed blue. I turned the hot water to its highest setting and let it run down on my hands. I knew it was hot because a stray drop would splash onto my normal skin and I would feel it burn. However, it didn't happen here.

Desperation caught up with me and I ran downstairs into the living room where the fire still burned. You know the rest of the story from here. My mother discovered about thirty minutes later saying she smelt something burning. I had no idea what I was doing until I heard her scream. One moment I held my icy hands above the fire to force warmth back into them with child-like panic, but upon glancing at my mother and back at my hands I saw blackened stumps.

The horror of the sight stuck with me. I never have seen burn victims before, but when I saw my hand, I was truly disgusted. Most of the meat of my hands was charred, the bone revealed and the fat bubbled and boiled, dripping into the fire. I was taken to the hospital, work was down on my hands, but I couldn't feel a thing. Eventually, it came down to an oblivious decision.

It is why I am telling you this story, so that you may record it because I myself cannot write it. The violin was in the attic, it never left and my parents never understood. It was sold to someone else, but despite the cursed item leaving our home I still felt a presence...a sense of fear embodied now in those rooms.

I don't know where that violin ended up, but I fear for anyone foolish enough to play it.

Rust and Spikes

"I don't know what makes you think we can fix this place up," I told Robert.

The warehouse was a strange mix of broken and rusted metal implements. It used to manufacture old war munitions, but that time has long since passed. The time between then and now, however, showed itself clearly in the decrepit environment. Of course, we still wanted the warehouse. It would also be a great marketing direction.

The warehouse would be scrubbed clean, and rebuilt if it was needed. We would advertise it as washing away the bad remnants of war and suffering. It would work, even if I had to pay a fortune for it to do so. I was making enough money off this financial adventure to do as I pleased, but looking at the warehouse I realized I would lose a lot of that income.

"Robert, I take it back," I told him as we walked. "There is plenty of space here, more than we would get from those other warehouses that we have seen. It is perfect for setting up the construction as well as a small division of workers."

It took a few meters before I realized Robert was no longer with me. When I turned around, I saw that he wasn't behind me, but making his way through the warehouse toward the exit

"Robert!" I shouted. "Get over here, we're not finished!"

Robert didn't listen to me in the slightest. I couldn't even see hesitation. Still, I wasn't about to be left alone in this place so I decided to join him and began walking after him. However, he had just left the warehouse when I was only halfway there. He turned to face me with a blank and fearful expression. In a second, he closed the door and I heard a metal clunk as he barred it.

I paused and stared at the door in disbelief. I jogged forward and tried the door, knocking, calling, shouting, and kicking. The door would not budge and despite the rust, it wouldn't break either. I went from feeling anger to fear as I turned towards the warehouse and began roaming amongst the machinery to search for another exit.

I would have used my phone if Robert didn't answer all my calls. There was nothing, but suddenly a glint appeared out of the corner of my eye. I turned to see a light had turned on near one side of the warehouse. With a small amount of hope in my heart, I walked over towards it to see it was a construction light pointing out a small set of stairs leading downwards into some sort of basement.

Most likely it was an area used for storage, so there had to be some safety exits; at least one maybe. I descended the stairs fully aware that my formal shoes were making loud metallic noises against the steps. Of course, what terrified me was the second last step. The metal broke and my foot shot through the step into something sharp, not to mention the broken edges of the step which bit and scraped their way up my leg. I yelled out in pain, severe agony running through my body.

There was nobody that would come and help me at this point. I pulled my foot off the metal spike below the step, thankful that it didn't go any deeper. Once I had done that, I bound my foot in a tie ridiculously. I cursed Robert for this. I would have him not only fired, but destroyed in the working world. His punishment will come later, now is not the time.

I limped onwards through another door to the floor below the ground floor. It was dark, but I noticed there were slits below the factory floor that provided enough light as well as the floor below my feet now. As drops of my blood stained the rusted grating, I wondered to myself if this place manufactured weapons as Robert said. The number of grates and saws led me to believe that I was standing in a butcher back kitchen.

My journey continued until I looked to the left. There were a set of stairs ascending and I believe towards the surface. Carefully as I moved, I soon reached the foot of the stairs. It was as far as I got before something loomed over my right side. I felt a deep cutting around my left shoulder and realized I had been struck with a saw blade by a large man clouded by shadows.

The teeth dug into my flesh and once they reached a no-go point my assailant wrenched the saw back, digging into me and sending me into a realm of pain I never thought existed. I felt sharp pains in my left arm that I would have thought were caused by a heart attack if it wasn't for the deep gash the monster created.

He raised his arm for another swipe and as it fell, I lunged towards him, pushing a shoulder into his stomach. The beast was heavily built, but I am not a lightweight. I felt the saw blade connect with my back leg as I toppled him to the ground. It wasn't the most painful fall for me, but more so for him. I quickly got to my feet and stumbled backward from my wounds.

The man lay groaning in agony as a dark iron spike of some machinery protruded from his chest. It was a large spike, not particularly sharp either, but the maniac had enough weight to help the spike drive itself through his body. He lay there, attempting to pull himself off, but the pain was too much.

It was time for me to leave, so within moments I made it back to the trap door and removed the bar. It opened easily for me, most likely due to the adrenalin. My car was gone, of course, no doubt it was stolen by Robert, wherever he was now. I limped away from the warehouse, always looking back in fear. I don't know why I did, that was a fatal wound if I had ever seen one.

I found people and safety. An ambulance collected me; a middle-aged man held together by makeshift bandages that the people gave me. It was a terrifying journey on the way to the hospital and I soon passed out. When next I woke, I was in a hospital bed surrounded by board members, hungrily talking about who would lead the company if I passed. Not a friend or family member could be seen. My life changed after that. I ran the company to the ground to stick it to those leeches that wanted to stab me in the back and as for the one who did, they didn't find a body, just a bloody spike.

Red Teeth

I enjoyed the camp for two reasons. One, I got to use the tent that took up space in my room, and second, marshmallows over a fire. However, this year's camp was the biggest pain because there was no tenting, only a cabin that I needed to share with twelve other campers. The marshmallows were yet to show themselves either. The worst part about camp though had to be the second-last night.

When we arrived at camp we first established where we would sleep and unfortunately, I had a bed that was the closest to a faulty window. Age had bent it slightly, so there was a small gap for me to see into the night. If I am being honest, I didn't mind initially. There weren't many insects in this forest and especially not this season either, so I could stare out into the dark without the threat of a bee or beetle flying into my face.

I would stare at the two things within view; the small, gurgling river and the dense trees. That is beside the point now, of course, but that river does become important later. The camp activities were fun and simple, but at some point, exhaustion hit me. I wheezed through lunch and made my way back to the dorm. One of the counselors could see how I was feeling and sympathized. She accompanied me to bed and wished me better health after some rest. I climbed into bed and slept through the day. Everybody went to the dorm and woke me up just as they were climbing into bed.

Once they were settling into the depths of sleep I climbed out of my bed and walked to the bathroom. After doing the business I began to brush my teeth, flashing a smile at the mirror. It was at this point I got a fright and examined myself more closely. Everything about me was regular. I had the fuzz of a beard, my eyes were okay and even my breath was fine, but some of my teeth were blood-red. I don't mean coated blood either, it was like red bone.

I brushed the red teeth and even scratched at them painfully to see if that helped get rid of the look, but there was some other problem. The teeth hurt a little, strong and new. My teeth were never this shape before. The red teeth were sharper and slightly larger. I brushed my teeth, still scared, and went to bed. I couldn't sleep well with these teeth. I kept tonguing them curiously and my greatest concern was if I was stuck with them forever.

The only reason I fell asleep that night was by convincing myself that this was some strange infliction or disease I never heard of and that it would be cured when I visit a doctor back home. Of course, it wasn't. Nothing about having new, red teeth was normal. Still, I slept easier after that and I woke up on the third last day. When I did, I kept my mouth shut and made my way to the bathroom before anyone else and checked my teeth to find they were normal.

I put it out of my mind almost immediately, blaming it on some bad dream. I felt a sense of relief that was so intense I smiled through the morning run while everyone else was groaning. I found a strength within myself and I ran much faster than the others, so much so that I wasn't picked last for the soccer teams. Truly a special moment, but while we played my aggression showed. I have always been competitive, but during that game, I was a force of nature.

Nobody wanted to challenge me when I ran toward the ball.

After that, we took a break for orientation on today's activities. It was a drag of an hour as the counselors explained the boring purpose of each sport or game telling us how they built character and showed us how to work as a team. In truth, nobody was looking at it that way. Everyone wanted to show some skill and stand out among the rest, nothing to do with teamwork.

That included me and that day I truly showed my athleticism. By the time the last activity arrived, I was the captain picking who would be on my team. It is safe to say that by dinner I was the talk of the mess hall. My mood was at its peak and it soon came time for it to come crashing down. One of the kids wanted to show me something he saw near the river, so I followed him into the dark while everyone ate or went off to shower. My friend knelt beside the river and pointed it out.

In the waters, I could see something pale at the bottom. It almost had a sickly glow and for a long while I wondered what it was, but soon the moonlight showed it for what it was; a body. It was torn apart, lacking in clothes, and held down with rocks. The face was terrifying, that of a female stuck screaming as her hair flowed around her with the current. My friend thought it was a dead fish, but once the moonlight lit it up, he gasped and gagged in horror. The body was severely mutilated, but recognizable as one of the counselors that greeted us at the start of camp, the one who walked me back to the cabin yesterday.

A wave of anger swelled up in me. I felt my teeth change within my mouth and I turned to the foolish child. My eyes felt hot within my skull and my lips parted revealing the gruesome teeth. I grabbed his shoulders and told him not to scream in a guttural voice. I felt the horror writhe inside of him as he saw what I was. I lunged forward, digging my already red teeth into his neck, ripping out his throat to silence him before he even could think of screaming. I began to rip him apart like I did the counselor and drag him into the waters, my body changing more as we sank into the darkness. Embracing the monster, the killer, the devil inside me.

I hid both bodies a lot better before returning to the surface.

I could feel it, the change, as I became more than human, more than mortal. I smiled.

Next Stop

I boarded the train and immediately started coughing. I buckled over, coughing into my hand and retching up the dregs at the back of my throat. It was a painful experience that made it impossible for me to breathe. There was one other passenger in the compartment and he ignored me plainly, staring at his newspaper.

Eventually, the inevitable happened and I collapsed onto all fours, coughing horribly. He finally looked up from the newspaper and decided to help me to my feet. He walked over holding his hand out and I took it. I was pulled to my feet and he slapped my back suitably until the coughing stopped. I spat the vileness into a handkerchief I retrieved from my pocket and walked over to a free seat, nodding my thanks with some softer coughing.

The man nodded to me in turn and returned to his paper, eyeing me with a measure of concern, but it was fleeting. I contained my disgust as I stared at the blackish blood that now spoiled the cloth and folded it neatly, tucking it away in my deepest pocket where it may not bother me. I rubbed the saltwater from my eyes and took the steady breaths that I lacked upon boarding. The night felt like it was to be a long one, so I opened my briefcase and opened the only book I brought with me.

It was a tale of mystery and investigation. A wonderfully intelligent detective was on the case with his trusted companion, a man who once was a medical officer in the War. A frightfully enjoyable read, although I must say that this 'Holmes' character is woefully egotistical. I read it almost unconsciously, falling into a state of quiet meditation, suppressing a cough or two every couple of paragraphs.

When that grew tedious, I began imagining myself inside the book.

I was at the crime scene, observing the body. It lay on the ground, sprawled out in a manner that hinted towards the man collapsing. A quick observation of the body and I realized that there were no visible wounds, which meant that the man died from more clever means. I began to ponder the possibilities in the dimly lit room when I was woken up by the sound of my book hitting the train floor and a hard thump.

My eyes fluttered open and I immediately retrieved it, looking at the man who helped me up. He had his arms crossed, the paper by his side, eyes closed, but not asleep. I believe he was imagining himself someplace as well, but realizing that it was rude to stare I decided it would be best to talk with him. After all, there seemed to be nobody else on the train and I longed for some decent conversation.

I waited until I saw him open his eyes before collecting my things and walking over to him. I raised my free hand to shake his.

"How do you do?" I asked politely. He stared up at me with tired eyes, but his pale body still had energy; he sighed.

"I am doing well, sir, but I must say you seem to concern me," he replied, referencing my episode. I held up my hands and pulled a smile with heart.

"Do not worry about me, it was a bad bout, but I assure you it is a sickness of my own doing. Too late did we learn how smoking affected our health," I told him; my hand was still raised to shake his cautious one. Eventually, he nodded in understanding and shook it simply as well as quickly.

I sat down beside him, minding the newspaper, and tried to pull my greatest amount of charisma and confidence to start a conversation.

"I've been investing in tobacco all my life and the irony falls on my consumer-based investments into tobacco," I explained. "Here I believed that by purchasing tobacco from the same brand I owed shares in I would soon receive a portion of that money back!"

I chuckled at the ludicrous thought and so did the pale man with a sad smile.

"And you, sir, what is your profession in these strange times?" I asked simply.

"Tourism," he replied with some steady nods. I eyed him and tried my best to picture him showing the French or worse, the Germans, where parliament was, but still, I wouldn't know what was best suited for the profession. He just didn't seem the right type.

"I see," I murmured thoughtfully. "And how does that treat you?"

"It was taxing at first," the pale man sighed with a sincere smile. "With time I got used to the strain and soon found enjoyment in it. A delirious kind of enjoyment, maybe, but now it is nothing to me. Something I do day-to-day."

"I can imagine it being taxing; definitely, but at least you meet interesting people. Tell me, do you often guide...Germans?"

The pale man laughed as whispered the last few words.

"I do, indeed. You would be shocked to hear how many I had to guide over this recent decade."

"Despite the war? That is odd...how many?"

"The war has actually helped my business. Millions of them, although I doubt that will make you feel better."

It was at this point that I was lost in his words. The pale man turned to face me and gave me a sad smile. His face was less tired, but more understanding. His face... was so familiar to me and it scared me deeply. The train trundled onwards for only a few moments before it began to slow.

"I believe this is our stop," the pale man noted. He stood up, collecting a paper I didn't recognize and an umbrella. "Come now, Gerald, you have a new world waiting for you. Don't fear what is to come; this is where you want to be and your parents wait for you."

I stood up slowly, realizing only now that my coughing had faded to nothing. I stood breathing fresh, pure air. I began to collect my things, but I realized I could not bring my old world with me. I nodded to the pale man and shook his hand one more time. Knowing now who he was, I wanted to ask him so many questions, but with a single look, he answered all of them.

I thanked him as we stepped onto the platform.

Inky Blood

I slammed my forearm down on the desk. Its metal was shredded, having been jammed in the door mechanism. There were definitely parts that needed to be repaired. Of course, the skills required were not in my possession. With my one good hand, I placed the head on the apparatus, sealed the container, and pushed a button.

I watched as the head was scanned, broken into, taken apart, and eventually compressed into a red mess. A small syringe appeared at the lower part of the machine, processed by the machine and containing a blue, neon liquid. I wiped the blood off the desk with an oily rag and clutched the syringe after. Jamming the needle into my temple quickly I shot the information into my skull. The nanobots began collecting the information and a portion of my mind went dark as it stored the skills.

After five minutes of fiddling with my arm, I suddenly had the ability to complete the repairs I needed. I took the tools at hand and began my work. I broke off scrap metal and began tinkering with machinations within. The technology began to whirr to life as I worked. I still had some adjustments to make to ensure it understood what I wanted it to do.

Eventually, my fingers began to move when I told them to. I used spare metal to rebuild the outside of my arm; soldering every corner and edge expertly as if I had been working like this my whole life.

I held my arm up and moved my digits. Everything was in place and working better than it did before. Now it was time to steal the face. My own was mostly electronic now, but with equipment around me, I could now steal the woman's face. It wasn't any more difficult than stealing her skills. I pulled a drive from the machine that crushed her skull and took it to the other side of the room. There was a surgical chair with several mechanical arms hanging above it. I slid the drive into place and the 3D model of her face appeared.

Lying down in the chair I began pushing the buttons in a sequence that not only changed the authority access from the corpse in the middle of the room to me but also started the process for my new face to be built. As the machine began to heat up I stared at my face on the viewing screen. There was only a metallic skull and cruel eyes. In an hour that would change. Once the machine was ready I sedated myself and let it do its work. A murky, electronic darkness awaited me in my sleep.

I heard the struggles of the past life belonging to this mechanic. The law is always out to get her. She provided too much help to the wrong people, but they could not pin her down. She was agile, smart, and innovative. She was always five steps ahead of any officer, making her a more brilliant strategist than anybody I had met. She cared about the downtrodden and hated the corporations. Her name, my name, is Angelica Doks.

When my eyes opened I saw a different face on the viewing screen. It was pale and fleshy and it had dark hair. Before I could collect myself and stand to my feet the restraints on the chair bound me. I was unable to move as the monitor descended. It faced the ground and a holographic projection of Angelica appeared. She stood before me and shook her head.

"I must say, I never thought I would bite the dust so soon," Angelica told me. "But I knew it would happen. You made the mistake of stealing...me...in my own home. I have contingencies that you are no doubt trying to remember, but can't. Let me tell you what is about to happen."

The hologram walked over to me and sat down on the mechanic's chair casually.

"Every night my brain goes under a deep-dive scan and my personality and memories and skills and whatever the hell makes me 'me' are placed into a powerful storage device just above this ceiling," Angelica explained pointing up at the dinghy ceiling. "Right now you feel your mind being cleansed of memories."

I immediately tried to recall the past, but indeed, I could not. Why am I sitting here and why am I so terrified?

"I notice you have stopped struggling around the halfway point, which means your purpose has been deleted as well," the strange woman told me. "These are your last moments before my mind is restored in your body. I must say, it is a fine body too. High tech, beyond anything you can find outside of the corporation. All fail-safes are disabled, easy as always, but now that your body is off the grid they will be coming here soon."

The stranger stared at me curiously before nodding to herself.

"You have no memories now, so you have no crimes either," she told me. "I will place you in a drive and send you to the corporation. I'm sure they would be happy to have a fresh mind to work with. Thank you for the new body, I've always wanted to go full cyborg, but it wasn't going to happen with just scrap metal. Enjoy the afterlife; I'm sure I will see you there."

***

Angelica removed the restraints once her mind had taken over her new body, she sat up meekly. In front of her was her fleshy body. It was bleeding massively from the wounds inflicted by the assassin. The weapons within her now were deadly and undetectable, which made sense considering how the assassin killed her without being scanned properly.

She climbed to her feet, feeling great. The strength inside of her now was immense. Her mind was restored, but the body was not her own. The experience of tonight will haunt her for the rest of her life, but Angelica had more terrifying memories than this. She walked around the room collecting her most important pieces, storing them in a slim backpack. Once that was done she began walking towards the door, only to stop upon hearing the surgical chair buzzing.

Angelica turned to see it eject a drive; it was steel, high-tech, no doubt belonging to the assassin. She walked over to it and plucked it from the machine. It had a small LED screen that displayed a single message.

"Please, I don't want to die."

Angelica read the message quickly and looked at the machines around her, feeling her assassin's presence. Their energy synergized with the electric hum all around.

"Don't worry...you never will now."

Disappearance

I work in the library of a quaint town a few miles North of the English Sea. The town was well looked after, with plentiful overgrowing plants and trees, delightful smiles, and an economy that is well-organized. Yes, there may not be so many people here, but we have more than the other towns adjacent to ours. We have a famous farmer's market once a week that keeps our town's name on the map, although barely.

The town's name is Conroy.

My job at the library wasn't enough to put food on the table, so I had to work part-time with the mortician, a truly dismal and sickening job most of the time. However, it was over soon enough and I could return to work, taking care of the library and continuing with my writing. A wonderful experience most of the time, but dreadfully dull the rest of the time. Inspiration was fleeting at most points, I'm sure you understand. However, there soon came a series of tragedies that filled me with such inspiration and I played a hand in these tragedies.

Not a direct hand of course, but I was involved with the bodies at the mortician. I woke up on what seemed a normal day and made my way over to the mortician to get the work over as soon as possible. However, along the way, I heard people discussing a killer. I asked what they were talking about and they informed me that three townspeople had been killed, one of the names I recognized was the retired butcher who lived in the center of town, not too far from where I lived.

My steps hurried me to the mortician and no sooner had I entered the town priest had left. He looked horrified, a worrying expression stretching his face into a sorry state. He gave me a nod as a greeting but walked past me without a pleasant discussion. He certainly was in a hurry, but what I found curious is why he was at the mortician's. I found out soon enough when I entered and made my way to the cold room. Dr. Jeffries stood at the middle table of the three. The bodies were covered, but not their heads. I recognized the butcher, not second, but the third I knew to be the priest's brother.

The doctor informed me that he had already finished the autopsy on all three and he was broken by what he discovered. The victims were killed by poison, but in addition to that, there were small incisions. Stab wounds as small as needle points, all over the bodies. The doctor told me he found it curious that none of them struggled at first, or were bruised or beaten in the process. It was only late last night during the autopsy that he discovered the insides blackened with poison, the toxic smell terrible, forcing the doctor to remove the stomach and seal it away in a container as well as a section of small intestines.

The doctor told me how this would hit the town, the panic, the possible-witch hunt, everything. For now, the bodies were to be kept until he could come up with a statement that sounded less terrifying than poison, violent stabbing, and a serial killer. While I was glad to leave the office for the first time since I started a part-time job with him I have felt a morbid sense of curiosity when it came to the bodies. Still, I decided it was time to force myself into more pleasant work. I felt a sense of excitement and anxiety.

Please, don't think I am childish or a bad person for feeling the excitement, I know how terrible the killings were, but the emotional shock they brought me also ignited a sense of inspiration within me which I used to continue my writing. A few days passed and there was no sense of panic or witch hunt as the doctor expected, however, the priest did apparently isolate himself during the days, at least until Sunday. He was in mourning, but his attitude changed, it was one of frustration and anger. Many could tell he was close to his brother, their smiles a common sight when they were together. The brother's wife tried to pray with the priest, but she herself was caught in an ocean of misery.

The spirit of the town was weakening, that much was clear, so I decided to take matters into my own hands. Now, I am not much of a man-hunter or even a policeman, but I know how to write. So, I decided to write an article for the town paper. In this article, I discuss the killer and my feelings for him. I made sure to include many insults and slander toward the supposed killer. It wasn't great writing in doing this, but it was strong writing that would hit hard, at least, that is what I hoped.

The priest contacted me upon reading the article and we discussed the killer. He told me my article showed too much anger, but he would not make me apologize. Instead, he shook my hand and thanked me. Something he would not normally do, but he felt it necessary. Sure enough, the killings had an impact and my article added to it.

Somewhere, in the town, there was a murderer who had been hurt in some way by what I had written. While I was intoxicated by the fifteen minutes of fame that I now had, I was also fearful for my life.

I told the priest my worries and plans to bring out the killer, knowing he most of all would most likely provide guidance on my actions, but once more he did not tell me if my actions were right or wrong. Instead, he told me to go to the police and inform them of what I have done and expect to happen. With another thank you and a stronger handshake, we parted. I didn't go to the police but instead went home. I do regret doing so and not taking the father's advice as soon as possible, but seeing as I am still alive, I cannot complain about what happened next.

Upon entering my home I noticed there were a few things amiss. For one, there was a noticeable smell in the air. It was the smell of burning, not the sweet smell of burning wood, but the terrible smell of burning foliage and plastics. I could not pin it down, but I had smelt something like it before. What mattered most however was why this smell was coming from inside my home.

I had entered my home quietly enough, the dark covered me from sight, but I still felt vulnerable. As if there was a huge target painted on my chest and someone stood somewhere in the house with a gun ready to fire the first shot. Still, this was no time for fear and I pushed forward into my home, making sure to not step loudly or turn on the lights. If there was indeed someone in the house I would be prepared to face him or her. In the end, I walked through the house and there was nobody to be found. I called the police in a hushed call and collected a weapon in hand.

Waiting is the worst cause of fear. Allowing yourself to wait means accepting something is wrong and in the time you have your mind begins creating worse scenarios than is likely. I felt it though, the grip of death closing around me as if the killer was in my home, hiding in the smallest impossible space behind me with a knife less than an inch from my vulnerable neck.

Luckily, my death was not on that very night and the police did arrive soon after my call for help. Once they arrived we proceeded through the house and began searching every room one-by-one. There is no doubt in my mind that somebody had broken into my house and we received the first and only sign of it in my bedroom.

Upon entering the room I saw a symbol had been carved on the wall above the head of my bed. It was four lines and the meaning behind it was clear. There were three deaths in the village and mine was to be the fourth. It was a chilling sight, but now the killer had made themselves very vocal in the community. What is more, the killer showed that my article had actually worked on them. I explained to the police that the one who wrote the article about the killer was me and they immediately understood the threat the killer had placed on me.

Considering the killer had poisoned his victims the police immediately seized any consumables in my household and cut the water. Everything would be checked for poison, but in the end, I would be better off buying a new batch of food. It was a frustrating, but necessary process. I went with the police to the station to help write a report while one of the officers stayed behind to watch the house.

The night never seemed to end and I doubted I would be able to receive any sleep. I was asked to stay with somebody I knew, but I preferred the comfort of my own bed. Even if I would sit in my bed uncomfortably watching the door and window at least I was in my own home.

That was exactly what I did, but instead, I paced in my bedroom, flashing a look at the carved tally on the wall and at the police officer that sat in his car trying not to fall asleep outside my window. Eventually, the light of day dawned and I certainly didn't feel too ready to tackle the day. I grabbed a purse of my money and decided to do some security shopping. I bought locks and bars for every little thing inside my home and decided to spend the day installing every single one.

The locks were strong and of great quality, but I knew this behavior didn't paint a good picture of me in the killer's eyes if they were watching. So, in my free time, I once more took up the typewriter and began writing a column around the killer. What I wrote was a lot more reserved, but in the end, still insulting towards my would-be assassin. It was too late that day for the piece to reach the newspaper, but I took it out all the same and delivered it to the printers while I also bought my food.

Upon returning home I saw the priest standing outside his church staring out at me. There was deep concern in his eyes and decided to ask him why. He only shook his head, telling me he saw the look on my face as I entered the printers. He told me not to stoke a fire too high as it may consume me, but I retorted that I would not be the one consumed. Indeed, my logic was sound and we parted on a forced farewell.

Once I was home, I did my rounds through the house, locking the doors and windows and making sure everything was secure. Once that was done I proceeded to my kitchen where I began cooking to my stomach's relief. I ate a meal that wasn't all too splendid, but it certainly was filling. I sighed, leaning back once more in my chair and eyeing the rest of my groceries. There was something truly sinister about a man willing to spoil good food in order to kill someone, but that was no longer my problem. What did concern me was the wine I had purchased. It was an older bottle, that was for sure, but what bothered me was the top of it.

The top of the wine bottle seemed fresh, almost as if the wax was burnt recently. I took the bottle in my hands and ran my thumb across the top gently. Upon lifting my thumb I saw some of the wax had shifted with ease and my thumb was stained with coloring. The bottle had been tampered with and with that in mind, my fear became truly real. I lifted the phone to call the police once more, but to my dismay, the line was cut and I felt the room turn silent as I heard a creak from the other side of the house. The footsteps of Death itself approached me.

I hid in a far corner of the room, out of sight, but I knew it would only take a moment for the killer to find me. Once hidden I waited for the approaching steps to reveal the face of the murderer. Sure enough, the light gave me the answer I sought once the well-featured face was brought to the surface from the dark.

The priest stood at the entrance to my kitchen, scanning the ground for my fallen corpse, but there was none. The elderly man which I had known for so long wore a face of dismay. I could barely contain myself and emerged from the shadows, a tall and stronger man than the priest.

"It was you who...but..." I stammered as I surprised the priest.

"Be gone child of Satan," the priest whispered in disgust at my sight. "How can you who have drunk such poison still stand to speak here now?"

"I did not drink your unholy wine," I spat walking up to the priest.

He tried to escape, but he only had the body of a frail man. I clutched at his wrist and then at the other which held a bible.

I threw him toward the front door and he stumbled on his feet.

"Curse you, child," the priest blurted in fury.

"Why did you kill those people? Why your own brother?"

"I did not murder anyone," the priest shouted. "I gave them a chance to prove themselves in the eyes of God, delivering them a vial of the most holy wine from my garden laced with the spirit of foresight."

"Spirit of foresight?" I asked. "Is that what you call arsenic? You are a murderer, old man! And a rotten liar. You will burn in the hell you have preached unto this town."

"The only one who shall burn in the black flames is you!" the priest shouted, lunging towards me with a knife.

It was so unexpected, but I was still faster than the old man. I grabbed the arm which sought my death, pulling the priest close, and tried to restrain him. It proved easy enough and I soon sat atop the priest. He began to beg for his life as if I was going to kill him then and there. The screaming was immediately silenced by a knock at the door.

I climbed to my feet and jumped toward the door, unlocking it and pulling it open. To my great fortune, it was a policeman, the same one who I had helped the night before. He stared at both me and the priest and after a few moments of panicked explanation, he decided to handcuff us both and bring us both down to the station with the bottle of wine.

I made my case half an hour later in the company of the priest. His behavior was different now. He seemed sad, concerned, and fearful. After my explanation, he explained an entirely different story which painted me as the killer and kidnapper. I felt that the way he explained his story was far more convincing and I soon realized that as a priest he certainly seemed a lot more reputable than a strange writer like me. I read it in the face of the officer and he was starting to choose sides.

It was an awful experience.

It was at this point I reminded the officer that the wine had been tampered with, and poisoned by the priest who had access to all the spirits that are offered by the spirit vendor.

"If I did indeed poison the wine, let me taste it," the priest said confidently. "I harbor no hate or malicious desires to poison anyone, so let me taste this unholy liquid, and let me prove it."

It was a brave statement to make and I was all too willing to let him try. However, the confidence he showed was disheartening, as if I was walking into a trap. I then remembered his words, telling me that the wine was 'God's test' for the people who drank it. The priest no doubt had drunk the wine before and lived. However impossible that could be, I could not let the priest win.

"No, I don't want to risk the life of a man, let an animal drink the wine," I told the policeman.

"There are other ways of testing to see if wine is poisoned, but if one of you is the killer you no doubt considered a way of hiding the effects. Luckily, I have a dying dog on which we may put out of his misery or at least ease his pain with the spirits."

Immediately the attitude of the priest changed as the policeman plucked up the bottle of wine. Fear flashed across his face and both I and the policeman noticed.

"Is there something wrong, Father?" the policeman asked.

"I...isn't it too cruel to use poison on a suffering animal?" the priest asked.

"On a better day, I might agree with you, Father, but his time has come and I would like to put this mystery to a rest."

The priest bit his tongue as the policemen brought his dog in and poured some of the wine into a saucer. The dog was indeed old and ailing, but I still felt a pang of pain knowing what would happen next. There was blood and writhing, but before the poor animal finally died the priest was thrown into a cell and my handcuffs were removed.

"The priest of all people...what would drive a priest to murder?" the policeman asked.

"His views have been twisted, officer," I explained. "I believe something has damaged his mind...perhaps an accident or chemical affected his mind...perhaps it was the wine he drank. Who knows, maybe if I drank the wine and lived, I would be like him."

"I hate to think of there being two killers in our village."

"So do I, but now we are down to zero once more. Thank you, officer...seeing what happened to your dog...I cannot express my gratitude."

"I always hoped he would pass in his sleep...I wondered what kept him alive so long and now I know why. At least God protected you, sir, and not one of his corrupt children."

"I appreciate your faith...but I don't believe God had anything to do with this...at least I hope not."

We left it at that and I soon returned home. However, at the back of my mind, I wondered how the priest knew which wine I would pick.

Loss of Sanity

"Can you please, just for the briefest of moments, shut up?" the Doctor yelled.

Yes, we were being loud during this session, but what did he expect? Personally, I prefer silence as well, which is why I don't speak, but how am I supposed to enjoy my silence in a place of mentally ill degenerates whose only thought is to prance around the place and if the mood hits them, dive towards an orderly and attempt to remove a vital organ with their teeth? There is no way, absolutely no way, no way in this life or the next will I ever forgive those that ruined my peace and now the Doctor was ruining mine.

It made me so angry to see someone who was a 'professional of the mind' lose his mind so quickly. How could he do such a thing when our futures depend on him? Perhaps he didn't care about our futures, but I was still getting a headache from his constant shouting so I decided to do something about it. I climbed out of my seat and ran towards him which I found incredibly difficult at first with the straight jacket on, but I made it there in good time and before he could react. Jumping towards him I grabbed a good part of his flabby arm with my teeth and bit down hard.

That is how I was thrown into the padded cell.

I enjoyed it deeply. There were no people and no sounds that would echo inside my head waking the voices up and telling me to do very bad things, very bad things indeed to all the people and animals that I could get my hands on. Oh, if only I could get my hands on something it would ease the anxiety a little, but in a padded cell, I had to make do with rolling around on the ground like the worm I was.

Two minutes or perhaps two years later I heard the alarms blare. So very, very, very noisy. It was piercing me even in my soft room. I started bashing against the door angrily to get somebody's attention and tell them to turn the alarm off before I tore them to shreds with my sharpest teeth. However, instead of the Doctor or an orderly, another patient appeared at the door and smiled at me beyond the strong glass. His teeth were not as sharp as mine, but his hands were free and he helped me.

The door opened at his will and he ran off into the corridors, leaving me to do as I pleased. Of course, there wasn't much I could do with a straight jacket on, but I soon found ways of ripping it off. There lay one of the secretaries not too far from my room, as still as a rabbit in my attic. I walked over to her and used her sharp nails to tear at my straight jacket. It was difficult at first, but she didn't struggle, perhaps from the blood loss and I had all the time I needed. In a moment, I was free and began my search for the lever that would turn the alarm off.

I ran as fast as I could.

Before finding the room with all the levers and buttons there was an orderly, alive, unlike the others I had passed. He was being attacked by this screeching woman, another patient who I had grown to hate in mere seconds as she yelled in pain and anguish despite being the one who was inflicting the damage. Of course, more noise is bad so I grabbed her and closed my hands around her throat. Within moments she was dead and I looked at the orderly. He sat there in the corner, staring at me with fear and tears running down his cheeks. Lucky for him he sat in silence, so I continued down the hallway and took lucky turns till I found the control room.

Inside there were two security guards, bickering amongst themselves, locked behind a door that was incredibly strong, far too strong for me to chew through. I watched them argue, but soon I grew tired and slammed my head against the glass. It got their attention and they raised their guns. Both fired at me without hesitation, but the bullet-proof glass protected me. I did not flinch or hesitate, but once they had finished shooting I pointed toward the bell just behind me which rang the alarm.

After this I clutched my head and grimaced, miming my displeasure. One stared at me without doing anything, but the other understood and leaned over to the control panel flicking a switch.

Peace.

The alarm had fallen silent and I stood in a hallway where the only sounds were distant screams and gunshots. Still, it was peaceful once I returned to my cell. I gave the security guards a positive gesture and mouthed my thanks before moving back to my room. It was a difficult walk back because of all the blood. I slid here and there because I was only barefoot, but it did not bother me. The noise was minimal and I enjoyed it deeply.

I soon reached my favorite room. The padded cell was an inviting stark white and I stepped in, dragging the body of the deceased Doctor who I found along the way. I closed the door and with a clunk here and there it had automatically locked behind me. I sat there in the center of the room. I could see familiar faces and their contorted expressions. I could hear the sudden fall of silence when the last victim stopped screaming.

I was overjoyed to tears as I sat, surrounded by gore and silence. It was by far the best asylum I had the pleasure of being in and I hope management doesn't change a thing.

Following Advice

There are many things to be said about 'signs'. I don't mean the ones left by the side of the road that tell you when to stop or keep going. I don't mean the ones that 'aliens' leave us in the crop fields. I mean the signs that life shows you when you are doing something right or wrong. Often, early in my life, like the rest of us, when we did something wrong there was somebody there to punish us. I don't know who is punishing me, but I know it is exactly what I deserve.

Her body lay in the basement, still as stone. I knew very well that I could not move the body, hide it, bury it, or anything. It lay there for nearly two weeks and every time I went down there and saw her I would fail in confidence and return upstairs. The smell grew too intense and it hit me then that the basement would be her final resting place. I worked the basement, coating the walls in a solution that would contain the smell. Every crack was fixed and covered with the stuff. Sealer and special paint had their own noxious smell, but they could not overpower the smell of the corpse beneath the tarp.

Once I had done that I sealed the doorway. My renovations went on for close to four days, but it was worth it. I had literally 'walled away' my problems, but even a man as cold as me could still feel intense displeasure in sleeping in a home that you knew housed a murder victim as well. Of course, I had to try.

I eased myself to sleep the first night but was confronted by the first taste of punishment. A nightmare that followed me wherever I went. In my nightmare, I was in my bed the same night. I scratched my head, and the grinding noise of nails on my hair filled my ears, but when I took my hand away the sound persisted. I held my head to see if there was something there, I tested my ears, but nothing could stop that awful noise.

The grinding soon turned to the sound of something sawing through wood. It didn't fill my ears now, it filled the room. As soon as it all began it stopped...and then I fell. The floor creaked and eventually buckled. The wood cracked as my floor descended down to the first floor. It only stopped me for a second and the floor broke as well. After the final back-breaking jolt, I was in the basement, bleeding from splintering wounds. Alone in darkness, but fully aware that I was in the room I sealed away.

I looked in the direction of the tarp and could see the shape of the body still covered. I moved my hands to push myself out of bed but felt them crossover something cold. Turning to face the pillow next to mine I saw her, cold, pale, and rotting beneath the covers beside me. Her deathly head turned to face me and she stared at me with the saddest, but most terrifying eyes I had ever seen.

I woke up screaming, no longer in my room. I was laying in front of the fresh wall that sealed off the doorway to the basement. I must have moved in my sleep because there was no way I would sleep there. The next night was the same, a nightmare with her, watching me. I could not take it any longer and decided it would be best if I escaped the home where it all began. I climbed into my car and drove till I couldn't drive any further. The nearest motel would have to be my place to sleep for that night.

Once I did find a motel I entered the lobby to find an old woman behind the counter. When I asked for a bed she began filling out a form. She asked for all the necessary information, name, and time of stay, but then she asked a question I stammered to answer.

"Reasons for staying?" the old woman droned.

"I...uh...I need a place to...sleep for the night?" I replied. I don't know why it was so difficult for me to lie.

"How many?" she asked.

"Um...one?"

"Where is she now?"

At this point, it felt like I was in another world. She was asking me where the body was...she was asking how many I killed as well...

"She is in my home basement...she is beneath the tarp...she is rotting and I...I can't sleep with her there in the house."

The old woman looked up at me plainly. She showed no fear of me or what she was hearing. She reached for the phone and began to dial.

"Wait...the door to the basement is sealed off...it's going to be hard to get in there."

"That is more than enough information," she replied, cutting me off with a wave. "Here is the key to your room. Try to get a good night's rest and we will deal with it while you sleep."

I went to the room, following her advice to the letter. How did I not pick up on the signs? I truly believed that this old woman was going to sort out all my problems and I fell asleep with ease. The nightmare didn't return, but that was because I was in another. When I woke up it was due to the police that were handcuffing me in my own bed.

I was escorted from my home as the police tore through the wall into my basement. I saw them gag from the smell as they pushed me through my front door. The neighbors watched as I was forced into the car and I sat there in silence as the policeman read my rights. According to the short trial that occurred a few days later, I had called 911 and told an old woman on the other side the entire story. I told her where I lived, where the body was, and how I did it...everything that I told the motel woman.

Since the woman could tell I was not mentally sound she ordered me to stay put as she took care of everything. It was the best advice I had ever been given because the nightmares would soon end once I sat in that 'special chair' the other death-row inmates talked about. I would close my eyes and fall into darkness, free.

To Be Prey

The most dangerous part of the jungle is the jungle floor. Many creatures that are basic prey have evolved to navigate the tree tops with ease. Hiding among the canopy turned out not to be the most simple decision as nature spat out another evolution of the snake that could grow large enough to climb trees with ease. I sat in a secure 'treehouse' inside a jungle and observed it all.

There was an incident in particular which I found most fascinating. I woke up early one morning in my sealed home and walked to the large glass window that allowed me to watch the creatures. There was one snake, in particular, I saw that was truly massive, it was hard to miss after watching the same set of vines and trees for so long. I couldn't help but think that a creature that size would be a danger to even larger predators, such as panthers. I was surprised to see I was more than accurate about this thought later the same day.

The snake had fallen still in order to camouflage a little better along the tree and branches. It was ingenious, but something I had seen a million times. What made this situation different was the jaguar that was wandering along the jungle floor. I collected a pad and checked the camera to see if it was recording. Once that was done I observed the snake as the jaguar wandered past. Eventually, it got so close to the snake that I was on the edge of my seat expecting the basilisk-size creature to lash out and attack.

It never did. I counted the jaguar lucky, most likely the head of the snake was somewhere else. Still, based on my observations of jungle predators and prey, the prey always learned how to defend themselves and the predator developed a new way to get its food. The circle of life repeats, but with each revolution there is evolution. Creatures change and adapt, although not as fast as plants, a lot faster than most believe.

It was when I moved to turn off the camera that I noticed the slowest movement out of the corner of my eye. Turning my head I saw the snake slither across the glass, ever so slowly. Once it had reached my end of the pane it lowered its head and its eyes seemed to meet mine for the briefest of seconds. I wondered how this was possible, it was one-way glass. I could see through, but it could only see itself. It was only when I looked closer towards its eyes that I saw that the color of its eyes was unlike any I had seen before.

In that instant I knew I wasn't observing a typical python, but rather an entirely different breed of snake. I marveled at its beauty for so long that I almost felt lost. The way it moved, the way it observed me as I did it. It was one of the most terrifying, but fulfilling moments of my life. To be so close to a new species, but at the same time, to be observed as if you were prey.

The snake continued to slither around the jungle area that I observed. A truly amazing find that I took hours of footage and made notes on. I knew for sure that it could not see through the glass, but it certainly was able to follow where I was. Perhaps it didn't use simple sight to locate its prey, perhaps smell, but I had the feeling it was more in-depth than that. I wanted to try something different one day to test out this hunch. I walked past the pane of glass and the snake eyes followed me closely. I then contained myself in clothing that protected my heat signature.

My hunch proved true because once I walked past the snake it continued to watch the same side where I left. It was as if I was invisible to the snake, but I had to test and see if it was purely heat signature. For the first time in years, I pressed a button that slid the first panel of one-way glass, leaving only a pane of two-way. I stared out at the snake and he continued to stare at that one side. It was incredible and terrifying. Truly an ability like that coupled with its size would make it the true king of the jungle.

I documented findings, day after day, and soon my interest grew braver than fear. I wanted to contain it, but I could not do it alone. I informed the organization, sent them the footage, and related my findings to them. I told them about the massive, new breed of snake and its extraordinary capabilities. Immediately they sent a team of their best hunters, armed with enough sleep darts to put several elephants to sleep and wearing suits that would hide their heat signature.

I was sent a tracker from them and waited for their approach. While I did this I kept the snake's attention. It observed me as I drank my coffee. I would have nightmares of it, I knew that much, but it was guaranteed when the team entered the observation area. The snake turned from me and dove toward the first hunter. His tail lashed out, knocking others to the ground. The entire area became alive as the full length of its body moved. I heard screams, each cut off with a chilling hiss and crunch as the sword-like fangs bit into each hunter, silencing them or paralyzing them for a slow death.

A cruel realization hit me; I had severely underestimated this creature.

The snake could see well enough, not just heat signatures. In essence, I was trapped in my box, with the world's most deadly predator coiling its body around my home. The snake's head returned, a snout covered in blood and a black tongue flicking out at me. I felt I was no longer an observer, I was just another victim.

Even though I was safe in the observation house, staring into the eyes of the snake, I felt I would die to its fang before I starved to death.

Being a prisoner is a crippling feeling in the beginning. At first, you feel helpless and almost suicidal with the thoughts that go through your mind. You are scared and worried about a future that you might not have. Those articles on prison riots started making sense. The prisoners grow desperate and frustrated; you see, in their agony, they wish to relieve their stress. How people relieve their stress is they resort to their most animalistic instincts in order to achieve cathartic pleasure. In a state prison filled with criminals, their base instinct is violence. When you are trapped in a chamber like mine by a snake so massive you cannot see all of it, you grow depressed and docile.

Reveling in this mental torture seemed to bring me comfort.

At least, that was what happened to me when I found myself trapped. I could have called for help, but what help I would receive would come in the form of paid zookeepers who didn't know any better. After a while, that ludicrous idea becomes your best and darkest option. I tried developing a better plan to escape, but I had none. So there I was, sitting in front of the large window, staring into the eyes of that massive creature and it replied with its own deathly stare.

I waited for help as I sat there in a destitute room. In my panicked state, I went through it, searching for any item or tool at my disposal that could help me, but I was an observer. The tools I had were purely for documentation purposes and nothing more. So, there I am, facing a giant snake only armed with a pencil, a few pens, and a stapler. Perhaps if I was an action hero I would have stood a chance, but I wasn't. I put my hopes in that of the professionals that would arrive soon that day.

There it was. A static bleep over the radio as the hunters informed me that they were drawing near. I gave them my warnings, but I knew what the result would be.

"Be careful," I told them. "This creature is fiercely intelligent and no doubt already knows you are in the area. You must watch every tree and even your feet. I will warn you when it moves."

"Roger that, sir," the hunter sighed. "Tell us this monster isn't as bad as you make it out to be."

"Your lives are at risk here," I told them honestly. "So do this right and we all might make it home tonight."

With that said I clicked off the radio and waited for a response. None came, which meant my words stuck. That was good, but that didn't change the result. The snake twitched and I knew straight away that it was about to make its move. I clicked the radio on and my calls to the squad of professionals.

"The creature is about to make a move," I hissed into the radio. "Be ready for anything, it strikes with teeth and tail."

The snake seemed to understand that I was warning them and left straight away not to give them a second. My opportunity was now. I leaped to my feet and dashed towards the door. I saw the tail of the snake flash as it slithered away. I knew the way out of this jungle better than any other, but I knew I would still be at a disadvantage. I pulled the door open after removing the safety latches and sped off up a path I always took.

I ran faster than I had ever run. It wasn't long before static came through on the radio, then silence, then screaming. The snake was efficient, it killed without mercy and saved its victims once they were all dead. I had seen it happen to the first squad, but that didn't matter now. The distraction was all that was needed for me to make it further away from this snake. The fools before made one mistake, they didn't run.

An hour later I left the jungle and was running across this open field. The grass wasn't too tall, which only made my escape that much easier. However, I believe my greatest motivator was when I looked back to see the grass behind me shift in a serpentine pattern. I could feel every drop of adrenaline burn my blood and pop my muscles as I ran.

I reached the first outpost that marked the border of the country. As part of the laws in the country, we had to be close to the border to conduct our research. It was for government reasons, but it basically meant if funding stopped we could be deported that day. For me, that was a gift. The outpost had other scientists and researchers who were expecting me with the team, but I simply told them I was the only one to escape.

I tell you, the looks on the guards' faces at the outpost...priceless, but certainly a suitable reaction. I became sickened with myself, my betrayal, my cowardice. It was murder what I did, but I chose to live that and tell a different story to the others. I requested the closest flight out of the country home. I was given it in less than an hour. The snake didn't pursue me beyond the field, I would have seen it and the outpost would have known.

The nightmares that the creature gave me were unique, but most of the time, exaggerated. The only physical feature that those nightmares remained true to the snake was the eyes. Something about those eyes even nightmares couldn't make it more terrifying. Now, it is two years later since I left that jungle with an email requesting that I return to service and aid in the capture of this snake for a large reward.

I do admit that by choosing me they would have the advantage of first-hand experience and I can provide details on the environment as well as the behavior of the snake, I am afraid that my firm and unwavering answer to this request was no, and never send me another email. My first encounter shall remain my last.

The same could be said about the others but in a very different way.

The Twisted Man

"A man in robes, a dark purple and orange," Dylan repeated. "Big fella, hunched over like this..."

"Sir, I think I would remember somebody wearing...robes," the store clerk replied lazily, unable to hide his disinterest in Dylan's search, but he still wanted Dylan to leave him alone. "Have you tried the post office? Everyone who enters or leaves this town has to pass them by."

Dylan sighed, not unhappy with the answer, but still finding a fury within him to fight the clerk. It was a feeling which was overwhelmed by the idea of meeting the man in the robes. The feeling was similar to returning to your home in the middle of the night to find it was broken into. As you check room by room, you are happy when you find nobody, but grow increasingly anxious with each room, as you don't know what you will find in the next one.

The longer you search the more likely you are to find what you are looking for. It may not be as you expect, it may be even worse.

Leaving the small gas station, Dylan thought back to when he first encountered the strange, terrifying individual. The robed man who has haunted him through the years.

***

While pedaling down the street back home, Dylan noticed an odd figure at the corner of the street. Hunched over, yet taller than his father and clad in dirty purple robes. Dylan remembered being so distracted by the figure as he neared it that he didn't notice the curve in the pavement. The front jerked, shocking him and causing him to tumble.

Dylan remembered an incredible pain, a hot flash of white stunning his mind. It was a pain familiar to every child. With scraped hands and knees, Dylan hissed at the foot of the robed man. The child, remembering the robed man, looked up at the figure, its silent silhouette against a sanguine sun. He remembered raising his hand to block the burning rays, only to be shocked by the monstrous face of the robed man.

Twisted, torn, with one eye and mouth too many, all mixed into a curved mass of flesh and teeth. It seemed so human and inhuman, so unreal. It was an unforgettable experience that filled the young Dylan with a unique disgust. Seeing the twisted man for the first time froze him on the spot. Dylan watched as the largest mouth spread in a vertical smile, only making Dylan's already contorted face grimace in further horror.

"Don't be afraid...," the mouth spoke so clearly that its words branded themself in Dylan's mind.

The words were whispered, calm, but the eyes didn't blink. Instead, they stared at him, ravenous, with the most malicious intent. Dylan found his feet and remembered how to use them at that moment, ignoring open wounds as he pushed off the asphalt and ran away. He didn't have a destination in mind, fear wouldn't allow such thinking. Like a terrified animal, Dylan simply ran in the easiest direction and did not stop.

It was closer to nightfall by the time Dylan reached home. Checking every corner slowly calmed his fear, making his way home on foot, he finally stumbled towards his house. As he neared it, he felt more secure, and safe. The freshly cut lawn, the comforting blue of the walls, his mother's figure moving in the window.

All the welcoming signs of home.

Walking into the house, Dylan breathed a sigh of relief. He joined his mother in the kitchen and listened to her talk about her day, from the terrible clients to the sweet old ladies who made her laugh. He observed his father and older brother staring transfixed by the television, a commentator relaying his excitement over each perfect pass of the pigskin. By the time he finally looked back out the window, it was just to catch a glimpse of the tail of the twisted man's robes.

Dylan ran to the window, but the man had already left, leaving Dylan's bicycle leaning against the mailbox. He did not sleep that night. Instead, he chose to check the window was latched every odd minute and his door locked every even minute. A delirium consumed him, tortured him, for many years until he grew out of it.

Dylan never saw the robed man again during those many years, yet the sight of him never left him.

***

"Hmm..." the post office clerk rubbed his chin.

Dylan waited, not expecting much.

"Yes, I recall such an individual," the clerk announced. Dylan's eyes widened, heart stuttering. "Fancy looking robes, old. Had a cane...or some sort of stick."

"Did he tell you anything?"

"He didn't come in here, just saw him walk past a couple of days ago. We get a lot of odd people coming through here."

"Leaving?"

"Coming. Must be a drifter and drifters like to eat; I'd ask around the diner in town."

"Thanks, thank you," Dylan nodded as he left, his eyes already frantic and darting.

Dylan was getting closer. It had been over twenty years since the day he first saw the twisted man. It was from listening to the radio one night that he heard of the man again. By mere chance, a chance which he could not calculate. Yet, it was the fact that he met such a unique man and heard about him again that made Dylan believe it was not by chance.

It was intentional, in some insane way, the twisted man must have known Dylan would hear about him on the radio.

***

"Tim, you must be joking. I won't have that, this is my show!" the host laughed.

"I'm telling you, this man was wearing wizard robes, straight out of the movies," one caller was telling the host. "Strangest thing I have ever seen and he was such a big guy too. I wanted to ask him what was up with the getup, but I couldn't get the words out. Didn' even look at me, just swung this stick and smashed one of my windows. I'm not a coward, but I'm not an idiot either. I put the pedal to the metal and the last I saw of him was in my rear-view mirror."

"What if the poor guy needed a lift?" the host joked, his sense of humor falling flat on his listener's ears.

"Not this guy, definitely not a hitchhiker," the caller replied. "You hear all these stories of people who seem so normal, but turn out to be…serial killers…or something. If normal people could be that bad, imagine strange-lookin' people like that freak!"

"Last thing you want in the backseat of your car, right?"

"That's right. I saw him on the road from Roxburg to Smithden. I don't recommend stopping anywhere near him, just keeping going. Stay safe out there folks!"

"Right, thanks, Tim, drive safe!"

***

"Yeah, yep, the odd one," the waitress replied. "All sorts of creeps come through here and he sure looked like one with that clothing, but he didn't cause trouble. Kept his head down, cleaned his plate, and didn't pinch my…well, he was probably the best customer I had."

The waitress laughed while Dylan read the nametag she placed strategically on her chest.

"Listen, Nicole, did you see where he went?" Dylan asked, in no mood for jokes and laughing.

"Why? What's he to you?"

"I met him a long time ago, I heard he was coming through the town and I want…to see him again."

"I don't know, hun, it doesn't work like that."

Nicole began to walk away but stopped when Dylan took out his wallet and pulled out a five-dollar bill. Through a not-so-subtle exchange, Dylan learned that the twisted man spoke with her. He told her he was going home, a mile out of town. Nicole didn't know why the stranger told her this, but he seemed intent on making it clear to her. She couldn't help but remark on how it stuck in her mind, finding herself repeating the words in the quiet moments.

That was all Dylan needed to hear to confirm his suspicions.

Dylan had come too far, he had to see it through. Climbing into his car, he followed the directions the twisted man had left for him. Seeing as it was such a small town, Dylan was on the open road soon enough, and later he turned off onto a dirt road that descended into a sparse forest. It made it easy to spot the cabin in the distance. It was no doubt the place that the robed man mentioned. For a brief moment, Dylan didn't feel alone in the car, but he ignored the feeling.

He was far too concerned with the sensation the cabin gave him.

Feeling the pull, Dylan stopped the car, leaving it without hesitation and walking towards the cabin. He didn't have fear in his heart anymore, he was transfixed by the cabin ahead. Had he kept his senses, he might have seen the several robed figures walking parallel to him in the distance. These figures faded into the trees as easily as they emerged and once more he was alone, standing outside the door.

Dylan made to knock, but the door simply creaked open, pushed by a gust of stray wind or pulled by sinister intent. For a brief moment, Dylan felt his mind clear and at that moment he wanted to run. It was the same instinct one feels when they are about to be bitten by a wild animal, the instinct that saves so many that listen. He stood in front of the gaping maw of the cabin and felt the fear of being consumed by the darkness within.

He could have run.

Yet, his eyes adjusted and he saw an empty, single-room cabin. At its center was the twisted man, standing, staring, waiting. Besides the twisted man, in the corner of the room, was a hatch, open and leading to some deeper darkness below. Dylan stepped through the doorway, unable to control himself.

"I...I don't...what...I..." Dylan searched his mind, but couldn't find the answer. Perplexed, afraid, but not sure why. With the man he feared for so long, standing so close, all Dylan could feel was lost.

The twisted man's hood bobbed up and down as he slowly studied Dylan. Dylan could make out his jagged smile, those gleaming eyes. He could see the glint of light caught in the saliva dripping from the man's fangs. The twisted man was happy to see him. Dylan felt catatonic, his mind struggling to think and his body struggling to move.

That was until the twisted man moved quickly toward Dylan. The speed, and the evil nature of this monster before him, finally helped Dylan's mind break the spell. He backed out of the cabin, turning to run, but immediately fell. Once more, Dylan found himself ignoring the pain as he scrambled to his feet.

Feeling once more like a child, fear flooded his mind. After cursing his carelessness, Dylan cried out for help, screaming from the depth of his being. It didn't matter. The twisted man gave him a chance decades ago, giving it to Dylan, and there wouldn't be another. Dylan had been chosen, he willingly stepped into the cabin and he would be dragged back inside, beneath its floor.

Stumbling once more, Dylan felt the twisted man's hands close around his ankles, he clung to the dirt, then the door, and even tried to claw into the floorboards, but it was all for naught. He felt his lower half descend and he twisted to see the dark cellar that the twisted man slowly sank into. Dylan's legs disappeared into the darkness and once more he struggled.

Only now, more hands shot from the darkness, they clung to his clothing and then arms. Dylan didn't scream, only cried.

***

Dylan's mother shook him frantically. Dylan was crying, then screaming, as his friends and other schoolchildren gathered around him. Everyone could tell he wasn't screaming over the scrapes on his arms and legs. He was screaming in fear, fear of his mother who held him and all the people around him. His face showed more and more fear with each face he saw.

Dylan was carried by his father into the family car. He tried to escape, kicking and screaming, fighting his older brother and mother in the backseat. Dylan's family were in tears as the youngest in their family fought them madly.

It was only when Dylan's eyes saw the robed figure walking away from the crowd, unnoticed by everyone, that Dylan fell silent.

He was silent then and would remain silent for the rest of his life.

Impostor

Habits are easy to develop if they bring you a sense of comfort. These can be good habits or they can be bad habits. Whether we like it or not, these habits define who we are in some way, to a point where even those close to us can subconsciously recognize them. A shift in character, even so slight, can be spotted almost instantly.

Jamie Anderson saw such changes in her husband, which grew into deep suspicion and eventually, she took action. Robby Anderson was a farmer in his late thirties and a hardworking man. Jamie noticed he came home late one day, but Robby didn't explain why despite her questioning. Of course, this is always concerning for every young wife. However, it began to grow darker with each successive night.

Robby would come back with a sterner face and grumpier demeanor. However, what bothered Jamie was Robby's change of habits. He never wiped his feet when he came home, but after his first late-night, he always did. He stopped drinking a nightcap, he started eating seconds, sometimes thirds. He even started watching Jamie's shows with her.

Small things that meant so much to her and for most wives, would be considered a blessing.

Jamie saw right through the new habits and decided to follow her husband one day. She followed him to work, watching him work tirelessly and eat his lunch in the company of his two friends. The three didn't say much, Robby especially. Eventually, the working day ended and everything started to take a turn for the sinister.

Instead of going home or joining his friends for a drink, Robby would drive his truck out of town and down a dirt road. Jamie kept her distance ensuring Robby didn't know he was being followed. It was dangerous driving as Jamie had the headlights off. Jamie knew that Robby could only be going to the river, which wasn't too far on foot. She stowed the car out of sight and followed.

Jamie told the police Robby met with many other people she recognized from town. Every one of them was digging a pit, wide and deep. Watching them so close became dangerous, as it took only one to turn in her direction and see her. She kept her distance, staying low to the ground, and waited.

Everyone dug without saying a word and at some point, they all decided it was time to stop. Everyone dropped their spades if they weren't using their hands and left in whatever vehicle they came in. Some simply walked back to town.

Jamie had to investigate further. She approached the massive pit and stood at its edge, staring down into the darkness. At the very bottom, she saw an assortment of objects, but it was too far and too dark for her to make out what they were. As she lifted her head, she saw that nobody had left and all stood at the edge of the forest watching her. Their pale faces seemed to be made of stone, but the feeling they gave her was not so neutral.

Jamie didn't spot her husband, but she only turned to see him swing his spade and knock her unconscious and into the pit. There was a snapping noise as she hit the bottom and Robby considered that to be the end of it.

However, Jamie lived.

Jamie awoke atop a pile of bodies, cold and lifeless. Her left arm was broken, but she was still able to push herself up with her right and examine the faces beneath her. Among them, she claims to have seen her husband.

***

"And that's when you decided to kill your husband?" the officer asked from the other side of the bars.

"No...that man was not my husband," Jamie told him softly. "I climbed out of the pit and walked back to town."

"With a broken arm?"

Jamie scowled at him.

"It wasn't easy, but yes."

***

Jamie made her way home on foot, ragged and in pain. It was nearly morning by the time she arrived, seeing the imposter sitting at the kitchen table eating breakfast. She considered confronting him or going to the police, unaware that Robby was the one who knocked her out. Jamie almost made the mistake of confronting him, but then she saw a woman in the kitchen with Robby.

Jamie's eyes widened in deep horror, the same way they did when she awoke on the heap of death. She saw herself, drinking coffee with the man that wasn't her husband.

***

"Aliens...demons...government conspiracy," Jamie whispered.

"Pardon?" the officer replied. "I didn't catch that."

"It was me...a woman that looked exactly like me with a man that looked exactly like my husband. I don't know how...I just couldn't stand there, afraid. I went to the shed, I found his shotgun and I shot them both through the window."

"Why through the window?"

"I didn't want to be in there, in case I missed."

The officer nodded with fake sympathy, but couldn't help but smile.

"What?" Jamie snapped.

"I've heard many stories in this line of work, ma'am, and I've only really started. Tall tales and bald-faced lies. Every one of them pleaded innocent with blood on their hands."

Jamie looked away, not wanting to hear anymore or waste her breath arguing. It wasn't until the officer turned the key to her cell and opened the door did she look back at him.

"Every one of them told more believable stories than yours," the officer continued. "Now, you don't seem crazy to me, or stupid, so I'm going to give you just one chance to show me some proof."

The officer placed cuffs around Jamie's wrists and led her to his car. He still put her in the back, putting a wall between the two. The officer was trusting, but not an idiot.

"Give me directions, show me where the pit is," the officer told her.

"What's your name?"

"David Rice," the officer replied with a smile.

"Take the next left, David."

Jamie fed directions to the officer and in moments they were going down the same dirt road that Jamie did. Rice helped her out the backseat and told her to lead the way, while she bombarded him with questions.

"Did you see the bodies? Of the...doubles, the impostors."

"No, not my job."

"What are they saying?"

"That you killed your husband in cold blood."

"And the other woman?"

"They didn't mention anyone else."

"What?"

"The only body they found was your husband, no evidence of another."

Jamie turned to look back at Rice, her eyes wide.

"She isn't alive," Jamie told him shakily. "Why would they lie and say I only killed my hu...that thing."

"My thoughts exactly. Doesn't make sense for you to admit to a double murder with there being only one body."

Jamie and Rice soon reached a steep decline, at the bottom, it leveled out along the river. There was no pit in sight, but there was evidence of one. It had been filled in, but the dirt was still fresh, forming a lighter circle, easy to distinguish.

"See? See? They tried to cover it up, but it's still here," Jamie told Rice victoriously.

David was already raising his radio, calling the station. Jamie approached him slowly, holding out her handcuffs. He shook her head, she wasn't getting off that easily.

"...hello? This is Officer Rice, can anyone..?" Rice began to repeat but was immediately cut off when Jamie wrenched his gun from his holster.

Rice reacted quickly, but not quickly enough. Jamie shot his leg, then his stomach. Rice fell, blood pouring from his wounds. It was at this moment that his radio began to crackle to life, hissing and squeaking.

David cringed at the noise as he clutched his stomach, trying to stop the blood.

"Yes, that's the last of them," Jamie seemingly told the air.

The radio hissed once more, this time louder.

Jamie stared down at David. His skin grew pale, but it wasn't due to loss of blood. He saw in her eyes everything Jamie told him about. An abnormal lack of humanity, a cold uncaring soul. He saw more emotion from the barrel of the gun in his last moments. The impostor pulled the trigger and her attention shifted the moment the bullet left the barrel.

Dropping the gun, Jamie began walking back to town, followed by other figures who were waiting in the forest. Only one was walking back to the pit, carrying the bloody, broken form of the real Jamie.

Another town had been replaced.

The Hunter

"Master Bennet will see you now, Mr. Fisher," the young butler announced with a false smile.

Mr. Fisher felt an incredible sense of relief as he left the hallway lined with the trophies of Bennet's hunting exploits. Being surrounded by such morbid displays did not fill him with awe or fascination, but rather a nervous discomfort. Almost as if Mr. Fisher were an unmoving witness to something evil, doing nothing to stop it, but unable to tear his eyes away.

As much as Mr. Fisher enjoyed a good hunt, he did not enjoy being surrounded by the prey's heads. He knew Master Bennet understood this, which is why his trophies were in his private wing and not adorning the walls in the public wing.

Bennet's office was much more laid back and fitting for someone of such stature. A foreboding office, but a comfortable one. A decorative carpet large enough to cover the floor softened Fisher's steps, but Bennet still heard him enter. Fisher could only admire Bennet's well-tuned ears.

"Fisher, how are the guests?" Bennet called from a dark room to Fisher's left. "I hope you're not like the rest of those stuck-up stiffs, turning your nose up at the food that was prepared!"

"Certainly not, sir," Fisher nodded towards the darkness. "The party is wonderful, the lights, the music and the food. Although..."

"Yes?"

"I'm afraid everyone is wondering where their host is. We all expected to see you at the entrance, perhaps even a speech."

"Oh, Fisher, you know that's not my style."

"And you know I am eager to begin. These people are only so enjoyable for a limited time, then they tend to grow on one's nerves."

A snapping noise escaped the darkness, like that of a stick being broken. Bennet's grunt was clear, which only caused Fisher's brow to furrow and his concern to rise.

"Sir?" Fisher stepped forward. "Is everything-"

"Just fine, Fisher," Bennet stepped into the light.

As expected, his attire was splendid, from head to toe. Fine shoes, onyx trousers, a deep jacket, and a startling white poet blouse. His face was clean-shaven and his eyes keen.

"Final touches and all that," Bennet explained. "I'm afraid I put the cart before the horse. I haven't prepared myself nor my mask, while my servants have done a wonderful job in preparing everything else. Now, down to business before we return to the party."

Fisher smiled, calm and ready for his questions.

"Now, the guests, how many do you suppose made it?" Bennet lit his pipe, taking small puffs to get the tobacco burning quickly. "I thought it was a tall order to invite so many."

"Apparently not, sir," Fisher explained. "Everyone could make it and with your reputation, they wouldn't miss it for the world."

"Really, Fisher, you make me blush. The servants?"

"All have their jobs it seems. The chefs work tirelessly, drinks are plenty, and food even more so. All are comfortable, easing themselves into their seats and enjoying this evening to its fullest. They will be sure to stay out of the way until the fun is over."

"It does my heart good to hear as much."

Bennet smiled warmly and nodded happily. Mr. Fisher knew what he was going to ask next, he always asked.

"You know you have my support all the way, Mr Bennet. Now, do you want to greet your guests?"

"Thank you, Fisher. That will be all."

His final word was sharp and cold, but Fisher didn't mind. It was simply Bennet's way when there was something else on his mind. Fisher still wore a calm smile, nodding towards Bennet before walking out of his office. Fisher knew Bennet's eyes were studying him as he left, the wheels in his mind turning like a clock keeping time.

"I like the mask, Fisher," Bennet called. "A wild cat...somewhat fitting."

When Fisher walked back into the part side of the manor, he found people just as he left them. Drinking greedily, knowing full well that if they were to pass out they would be in good care. Everyone was among friends, treated like royalty. The stresses of their life had long since melted away and now they were relishing in the luxury.

Fisher could almost see their inhibitions being abandoned.

From room to room, everyone had found their comfortable seat to warm. Fisher soon found his place in the first room that Bennet would be entering. Two fat men sat by the fireplace, the warm light highlighting their rounded features. Three women chattered amongst each other, complimenting each other's masks and insulting others.

As Bennet approached, servants vacated the many rooms as fast as they could, the music's volume rising ever so slightly. He walked through the halls, calm and ready. Fisher saw him approaching and announced to the room that the host was approaching.

The fat men rose, as did the woman with a bit more grace, but Bennet held his hands up, bidding them rest. Fisher smiled softly, studying Bennet's mask with everyone else.

A real wolf's head, clearly butchered with its jaw torn from the skull. A set of horns, most likely that of a young stag, stuck out from holes above the eyes. It was vile and sinister, making one man's stomach turn at the sight of it.

"Please, everyone, rest easy," Bennet smiled, his lips barely visible, but expression clear. "It's wonderful...so very wonderful! To see such dear friends, forgotten loves, and inspiring peers."

As he spoke, gathering everyone's attention, Fisher approached the closest victim, drawing a serrated blade. With powerful, cruel intent, the knife slit the first aristocrat's throat. Before anyone could realize, another victim hit the floor, a victim of Bennet's decisive thrust of a silver dagger.'

The massacre was quick, brutal, and over. The screams silenced quickly.

In the next room, a young woman with a feathered mask tried to leave to find a friend but was stopped by a butler who guarded the door.

"I'm sorry, Miss Atwood," the butler told her with a stony expression. "Master Bennet is greeting everyone room-by-room and wishes everyone to wait only a moment."

Atwood simply stepped past the butler who stumbled to catch her but didn't give chase, afraid of losing the many others in the room.

"It will take only a moment, you old fart," she replied childishly. "I'm sure Master Bennet won't mind too much."

Atwood skipped onward, peaking into the room where the first slaughter took place. It was quiet, the fat men slumped in their chairs and the three women spread on a single sofa. Not seeing her friend's brightly colored dress, the young woman didn't look too hard at the still figures and moved on to the next room.

As Atwood pranced towards the next room, admiring the drapes and sparking lights. That is when she saw a man stumble out of one room, wearing a wild cat mask.

"Excuse me, excuse me," Atwood sped towards Fisher, who was deeply shocked to see the woman out of one of the many smoking and lounging rooms. "I'm looking for a good friend of mine, a Miss Lorena Littlechild?"

"L-Lorena Littlechild," Fisher repeated, his shock breaking into uncontrollable amusement. "I believe she may be in this room, shall we?"

Fisher's smile coupled with the shaking hand that gestured to the room he just left disturbed Atwood. For a moment, she believed him to be a bad drunk, but as she studied his mask and suit, making out the clear marks of blood, she hesitated. A scream soon escaped the room followed by the screamer.

A tall man was brought to the ground by Bennet's tackle and immediately silenced by a knife. The evil that Atwood saw in the eyes of the horned wolf that Bennet wore was enough to make her faint on the spot. Fisher stared down at her crumpled form, raising his eyes from it to the heads that peaked around corners and out of the rooms adjacent.

"Master Bennet, I believe the jig is up," Fisher smiled with sinister humor. "A little sooner than usual..."

Another scream as the bodies were noticed, more as the blood spread across the floor. Bennet stood, with a bloodied dagger, eyeing every face. He was not angry.

"I prefer the chase," a hushed whisper escaped the mask.

Pandamonium.

Aristocrats, helpless and scared thanks to drinking and panic. Many fell on the smooth tiles, their heels, and hard shoes aiding the killers. Fisher and Bennet's cuts were quick, not meant to kill now but to slow down. In the chaos, many discovered the doors were locked. Some discovered there were no windows on the first floor.

One had almost broken a lock before he was cut down by Master Bennet himself.

The bloodbath was loud at first, but within half an hour it was silenced. Survivors hiding here and there, only to be found and promptly executed. The servants and chefs waited in the kitchen, beyond a locked and barred door. Terrified of their master, the servants prayed they would make it through another one of Bennet's hunts.

A few more hours later, the last scream echoed throughout the manor.

The servants unlocked the doors and began cleaning the manor, from top to bottom, saving the majority of the bodies on the first floor for last. Meanwhile, Fisher and Bennet took the register of the guests and began checking off names as they piled them together, checking beneath each mask.

"A fine night...a joyous night," Bennet announced as Fisher read. He breathed deeply, ignoring the aching muscles and injuries he sustained from those who fought back.

"Truly..." Fisher replied, crossing off the names. "A Matilda Parkes?"

"Yes, I got that one and a Lorena...ah, Lorena Littlechild. One of your additions to the list?"

"Yes, I met..."

Fisher's voice trailed off. He recalled the name and the woman who wandered out looking for her.

"A-Atwood...that girl...she fainted," Fisher murmured.

"Yes, I saw," Bennet nodded with a satisfied smile. "How terrible we must have seemed at that moment."

"Benedict, she is still alive."

The two cruel men exchanged looks before rising from bloodied seats. With rapid movements, the two took sharp corners till they entered the same hallway once more. Only blood and bodies of the victims that were crossed off the list, but no Atwood insight. Looking further, they saw one of the doors to the outside was open. The darkness of the night with its cold air brought with it a terrible fear for both Fisher and Bennet.

"It's only forest and mountain for miles," Bennet reminded Fisher. "I will collect the guns, see if you can make out some tracks."

Bennet left immediately for his room while Fisher ran towards the open doors. Opening them wide, he stared out at the forest. In a rage to see more clearly, Fisher tore his mask off and scowled. He heard footsteps behind him too late, turning on the spot to see the murderous intent in Atwood's eyes as she drove an antique sword through his cold heart.

"Y-you monsters..." Atwood whispered at first, but her voice grew louder as confidence grew. She brought Fisher to the ground, twisting the sword, wrenching it from his torso, and striking again and again with each word. "Demons...traitors...murderers!"

Fisher died with the first strike, but the words followed his spirit in its descent. Atwood glared a tired fury into his empty eyes. It was the metallic click behind her that brought her back to reality. Turning around, her eyes rested on the bloodied figure of Master Bennet, although none of the blood was his.

"Remarkable, Miss Atwood," Bennet aimed his rifle at her. "I didn't think you had it in you."

The hammer clicked, but no bang, a notorious fault in the rifle's making. Atwood sprang to her feet, Bennet drew his dagger. Despite him being an experienced killer, Atwood's sword was more difficult to dodge. The blade ran through his center, his dagger piercing her side. It was a test of wills and Bennet's won at first.

Miss Atwood collapsed to the ground, passing on during the fall. Bennet fell to his knees, then fell onto his side. Unable to move, he stared at the feet of the many victims along the hall, the pools of blood. The dark eyes behind the evil mask grew darker as he died smiling, knowing that what happened that night would be remembered.

That a part of him, a nightmarish memory, would live on.

The Vessel

The ship raised anchor on the shores of a dying island. The crew could not understand why the captain would go ashore in the first place. The island appeared to have suffered fire and flood. Ashen trees and rotting ones littered the sand, fuming in their ways. It had an aura of death, disturbing the superstitious deckhands. All were happy to see the captain return, happier still to hear the orders to weigh anchor and sail away.

Yet, the question was raised why the captain would want to go ashore. He was a man of sensible nature, which was more than could be said for most of the crew. He returned empty-handed as well, at least, it appeared that way. Questions such as these gave the crew reason to watch the captain closely but were left staring at the door to his quarters.

"What is he up to?" one foolish crewman asked. "I sense mischief..."

The others turned angrily towards the fool, one grabbing him by the front of his shirt. The crew demanded respect, as the captain had earned theirs with every action since serving aboard his ship.

The fool apologized bitterly but sincerely regretted mentioning it. Yet, the fool simply said what was on every man's mind. The crew hated themselves as much as the fool, as they couldn't help but agree. Most decided to brush it off as it never happened, but others decided to take action.

Two crew members discussed the island in-depth, sharing superstitions and stories, their twisted fear concocting a greater horror with each story. Their restless hearts could take it no longer, and both agreed to spy on the captain later that night. Sneaking out was easy, and avoiding the quartermaster was difficult, but both reached the captain's door.

"Wait," one whispered as the other reached for the doorknob. "Come here."

The second joined the first in peering between curtains in a small window. It was uncomfortable, but both were treated to a dark view of the inside. Not a candle was lit, not a lantern burning. Instead, a flash of light surprised the two, illuminating the captain at his desk.

Thunder rumbled as the two deckhands tried to calm their hearts.

Returning to the window, they could now just make out the captain's silhouette in the darkness. He didn't move an inch, he didn't even seem to breathe. The sight of their still captain only worried them, as he was in such a position that he couldn't be asleep. Superstitious fear could not hold them back, they had to know that their captain was alive.

Without hesitation, the two opened the captain's door and marched inside. Greeted once more by the flash of lighting, the two could see their captain's eyes flashing white. One, the most fearful of the two, fell back in surprise, backing towards the door. The bravest stepped forward, examining the captain from across the table.

"He is dead," he murmured. "His eyes have rolled back...he is so pale."

The two approached their captain's body, feeling a pang of sadness, but dark curiosity. Looking down, the two noticed an open box in front of their captain. Leaning close, one could see it was a crude box, sitting on a dirty, ashen cloth. The only clue of what was inside was the fade of the wood in the shape of a circle.

"We must tell the others," the deckhand murmured.

"No, are you crazy?" the fearful one stammered. "I would be the first one the crew suspects. Let's leave him for someone else to discover."

Without waiting for a reply, the fool left in a hurry, returning to his hammock below the decks. The second was tempted to tell everyone, but once more, the fool's words filled him with fear and he too left without a word. The two joined the sleeping crew safely, their nighttime adventure unknown to all, but each other. Both could not sleep, but soon the exhaustion of the day caught up with them, just before dawn.

The next day everyone returned to their posts, taking care of the ship and cleaning when they had free time. It seemed like an average day, one where nothing strange would happen, yet the two deckhands found themselves eyeing the captain's quarters. The door remained closed, nobody discovered the body.

It was only around midday that the 1st mate approached the captain's door. The deckhands watched from afar as the 1st mate knocked on the door.

The door opened, to reveal the captain, alive and well. The captain spoke with the 1st mate, marching out on the deck, scowling at everyone like he normally did. The captain marched up the stairs to the helm, speaking with the quartermaster on what appeared to be the heading.

What terrified the deckhands most was the lack of any unusual behavior.

"I thought you said he was dead," the fool hissed to the second deckhand.

"He was, he was cold, pale, everything!" the other replied. "Now he is alive, like some sort of gh-"

The deckhand fell silent, exchanging a look with the fool. In their hearts, a fear crept pure and true. It made perfect sense in their minds, but they could not see proof, nor tell anyone of their suspicions. Discussing it amongst themselves, they exchanged ideas on what they could do to be rid of the ghost.

The deckhand suggested a special brew, but the idea was crushed by a lack of knowledge on how to make the brew or give it to the captain. The fool then suggested they throw something at the captain, see if he was solid as a man, or immaterial like a ghost. It was an idea that did the least harm, so it was the one they stuck with.

Taking an apple from the cook's pantry, the fool returned to the upper deck, walking casually towards the captain. The deckhand watched closely as the fool greeted the captain, stuttering with slight fear, before offering the captain an apple. Before the captain could answer, the fool tossed the apple in the air. The captain caught it with a grin, taking a hearty bite and thanking the fool.

"I am more confused now," the deckhand murmured.

"What's confusing you?" another deckhand asked.

"N-nothing, just...nothing."

The captain coughed, spluttered, and choked. The scene frightened the fool as the captain coughed up the apple, spitting blood onto the deck.

"Poison!" the captain choked.

The captain clutched a pouch of medicine in his pocket, begged for milk, and drank it deep when it came. The medicine seemed to take effect, but the captain's skin became a frightening shade of green before returning to normal.

The fool was grabbed by the other crew while the captain tried to stand tall. The fool pleaded innocence, but the proof was damning. Even the deckhand was in shock, realizing he must have made a big mistake. The fool tried to explain, pointing at the deckhand who joined him the night before.

Yet, the deckhand explained it must have been fear that made him see those things, fear that clouded his mind. He explained how he had nothing to do with the apple, the other deckhands vouching for him, saying he was on the upper deck the whole day. With those statements, the fool's safety line was withdrawn and he was at the mercy of the captain and his furious crew.

The fool stared up at the captain, trying to explain how he didn't poison the apple, but the words fell on deaf ears. The captain drew his sword, shifting the coat he wore for only a moment. The coat shifted enough for the fool and deckhand to see a round amulet, made from bone and black feathers. For the briefest moments, they could see a smile twitch on the captain's face, his eyes flashing white, as he stepped forward.

The captain's sword drove through the fool's heart, blood spilling on deck until his body was thrown overboard. The crew felt a lot better having been free of the fool's superstition but were worried about their captain.

The captain walked towards his quarters, stopping in front of the door and turning back to his crew. He bid the deckhand join him, with a sinister smile misconstrued by the rest of the crew as a forgiving one. Without the pressure of everyone around him, the deckhand walked into the captain's quarters, swallowed by the darkness as the captain shut the door behind them.

The crew forgot the deckhand and the fool, unintentionally damning themselves to become a dead man's crew. All the while, their minds thought they served under a simple captain, not the Ferryman of the Sea, the Dread of the Damned, the Davy Jones reborn!

The Devil's Contract

The office was an oddity in itself. A long table, two chairs oneither side, and no windows. The room was lit by fluorescent lights that gave everything a sickly tone. He came in through a door at the end of the room, sat in his chair across from me, and stared into my eyes. He turned the room from sickly to sinister. Of course, he did. When it comes to signing this contract what happens is serious, but at least effective.

He had nothing in front of him, yet after seeing me all he could do was look at the tabletop. I found this unusual, it would make more sense if I avoided eye contact with him. Perhaps this wasn't him and was just a representative. I immediately felt more confident and a little aggressive. I stared daggers at him.

"What do you want?" He asked in a tired voice. The voice didn't echo in the bare room, it just cut across the massive table straight to my ears.

"I need money," I replied.

"That's not what I asked you."

He raised his eyes again and my mind fogged up. It was hard to tell why, but I now had the answer. Perhaps he needed me to be more descriptive, but money is so simple. How could I describe it better?

"I want a lot of money," I told him.

"A fortune to keep you and those around you happy for the rest of your life?" He suggested. It was what he was looking for, a better answer to put on the contract I suppose.

"Yes."

He looked down again.

"Sign the contract and it will be done." He told me.

I looked down and saw a sheet of paper. At first, I didn't understand the strange symbols, but as if it read my mind the page shifted out of reality and returned bearing the Italian language. I blinked twice and there was no evidence to say it wasn't Italian before. Immediately I began to feel nervous, but I tried to persevere. Did he know it was now false confidence?

I began reading the contract and the room grew tense. It was as if all the forces around me wanted me to hurry up and make a decision the moment I read the first word. I gave in and quickly scanned the document. All I saw was benefits and nothing that suggested a loss.

Every line was not a promise, but a guarantee of all my desires being fulfilled. There was more to the contract than just talk of wealth. There were guarantees of more sinful desires and my heart began to leap out of my chest as I imagined it. I could practically taste long-lasting happiness and I smiled to myself, completely forgetting about him on the other end of the table watching me.

Satisfied I reached for the pen beside the page. It was a strange pen and I knew from picking it up I needed to dip it in ink. Again, as if reading my mind a small bottle with ink appeared by my side. When I dipped the pen into the bottle the ink turned red and my head felt lighter. I looked up to see he was looking at me. Watching me with a stone-cold face that told me everything I needed to know.

The ink vial did not contain ink, but my blood. Somehow I felt that a lot more was taken from me than the vial contained and I felt a lot weaker. Still, I persisted to stare back at him until he backed down, but he didn't, he would never. Why would he? I was a fool and I saw it now. The powerful fear I felt was akin to that of a fly in a spider web. I felt hot and my skin began to itch as my heart raced.

I couldn't do it. Everything about this felt wrong and my desire for money grew a hundredfold. I was suffering from inner turmoil about choosing my fate. If I didn't calm down I would have to leave. He was already deciding what to do with me once I signed the contract. I could no longer see his face, his whole body was somehow caked with shadow despite the light above him. I felt a cruel smile in that darkness.

"I...stop looking at me," I replied, staring across the room at him.

He was me, well, he looked like me. He was me if I signed the document, happy and expecting. Then he was me if I didn't, poor and angry. In a rage, a rage so powerful after seeing such trickery, I picked up the vial of my blood and threw it at the suited man who sat there.

The bottle shattered against a surface in between us. I didn't see anything between us until now, but this time I could see it was a glass pane. It began to crack and the left side began to fall apart. Shards peeling from the frame and shattering to splinters that could pierce you right through. I saw the room behind the glass and it wasn't what I saw through the glass. There were now only a few spots of paint, which came into view only when the fluorescent light flickered on.

The glass began to fall from the left side toward the right slowly. I saw the now decayed room, decrepit, and his half of the table completely shredded as if claws and teeth had torn at it. The dirtied fluorescent light cast an off-gray light when it flickered on, my heart stopping every moment it went dark.

He stood up and began walking towards the door. His steps weren't the defined click of fancy shoes now, but the fleshy thumps of bare feet. I couldn't move. When he reached the door he looked at me again, glass falling off, getting closer to him, soon to reveal his true form.

Before it did he flicked the light switch, plunging us into darkness before I could see the monster. I heard the door shut and I was alone. I stood up and made to leave, reached the door, and pulled it half-open before I heard a click behind me. Glancing back I could see the room back to what it once was when I first arrived. Glancing down the table I could just make out my signature on the contract as it burned out of existence.

Other Books

Written by Matthew Dewey